THE SHERIFF FINDS A FIANCÉE

The Stevenson Brothers - Book Three

ANNABELLE MARIN

Published by Blushing Books
An Imprint of
ABCD Graphics and Design, Inc.
A Virginia Corporation
977 Seminole Trail #233
Charlottesville, VA 22901

Annabelle Marin
The Sheriff Finds a Fiancée

Print ISBN: 978-1-63954-224-6
v1

Cover Art by ABCD Graphics & Design

Chapter 1

Peter Stevenson always thought he would be married, perhaps with a baby or two, by the time he was thirty-eight. Yet here he was, nearly forty and still living the bachelor life. Working at protecting the fine town of Redwood as the sheriff, of course, but also drinking and flirting with women. He loved women. He liked their soft skin, their curvy figures, and the way they looked at him with mischievous looks on their lovely faces.

Though, lately, Peter was feeling restless. Not unhappy per se, but certainly discontent. Almost as if something were missing. There was only so much flirting, drinking, and rolling in the hay he could do before getting bored with the process. He *was* pushing forty, after all; it wasn't like he was a young man of twenty-one anymore.

Maybe it was because he was the only Stevenson brother who wasn't married. His younger brothers Derek and Stefan had married two years ago, in 1880, and were now proud husbands and fathers. Stefan had taken over

1

the family ranch and he and his mail order bride, Imogene, had welcomed their first child, a daughter named Daisy, in July. His other brother, Derek, was a pastor, and he had married a young woman named Penelope who had been disowned by her parents after nearly running away with a man who did not have the best intentions. Penelope had just given birth to a baby boy they'd named Colin.

He loved his brothers, his niece and nephew, and his sisters-in-law dearly, and they had never made him feel unwelcome or unloved. But lately, whenever he looked at his brothers with their families, he felt his chest swell with jealousy. It was almost a longing; he wanted the love they shared with their wives. He wanted a family of his own. But how did one go about acquiring a wife? Stefan had ordered his, and Derek had picked his up like an abandoned kitten. Many women in town flirted with him and he was always eager to flirt back, but to be honest, he couldn't remember the last time he had courted a respectable woman—probably in his twenties. He did, however, remember he had acted like a fumbling fool.

Perhaps he would ask his sister-in-law, Imogene, to pick a bride for him. She had offered before, but he had never taken her up on it. He had always assumed there would be plenty of time to find a girl to marry, but suddenly everyone seemed to get younger, and Peter just felt *old*, even though he was stronger and more skilled than men half his age. It also didn't help that he was thirty-eight and had moved back in with his *parents*.

It's only temporary, Peter grumbled to himself as his mother, Mrs. Bonnie Stevenson, whacked him on the shoulder because he had sat down in his dirty work clothes on the expensive love seat she and Imogene had just restored.

Peter had his own house in town, but there had been

some horrible winds, causing many buildings in town to be affected. His house had, unfortunately, been one of them. Three heavy tree branches had landed on the roof, causing it to cave in and making the house unlivable.

Even though he was throwing out plenty of money to get it fixed, the workers he had hired told him the damage was extensive enough for repairs to take at least a month. Derek and Penelope had offered to let him stay with them, but they had just had a baby and he didn't want to intrude. Imogene and Stefan lived too far from town, so off to his mother's, he went.

"Wash up, dinner is ready." Mrs. Stevenson tapped him on the head, making Peter feel as if he were eleven years old again. It was only his mother and himself in the house. His father, Isaiah Stevenson, had gone to Milwaukee to visit his recently widowed brother for a month. "I just received a letter from your father. He arrived in Milwaukee all right."

"How's Uncle Timothy?"

"Sad, as you would expect; he and Gretchen were married for over twenty-five years. Hopefully, your father will be able to cheer him up a bit."

After Peter had washed up, his mother fixed him a huge plate. She was convinced that because he wasn't married, he was starving every night, even though there were plenty of cafés and restaurants in town. "I need you to go to the train station the day after tomorrow."

"Why?"

"After Miss Smith left town to marry, the school board put out an ad for a new schoolteacher. She's a young woman coming from New York. Her name is Miss Bethany Fields. She was originally going to board with the Meyer family, but after poor Mr. Meyer died in that terrible accident last month, Mrs. Meyer decided to go back to her family in Virginia. Mr. Ingalls, the head of the school board, asked your father and me if we would give Miss Fields room and board, so she didn't have to constantly stay with different families the way it's traditionally done. I need you to pick her up just in case she has heavy luggage."

"Isn't that the head of the school board's job?" He was a busy man; he didn't have time to pick up and get the new schoolteacher settled.

"Mr. Ingalls can hardly walk without his cane. Surely, you can't expect him to greet Miss Fields by himself. I promised him I would give her room and board while she stayed in Redwood."

"For an entire school year?" He raised an eyebrow. Having a guest who didn't leave, would annoy him.

"Yes. She's a city girl, so we'll see if she lasts the entire year." An amused smile played on her lips. "Now that most of you are up and married, your father and I are a bit lonely. I miss having another woman in the house like when Imogene and Penelope stayed with us briefly."

Peter narrowed his eyes at her. "This isn't a match-making scheme, is it?"

Mrs. Stevenson snorted. "Don't be silly. You and your brothers made it perfectly clear you didn't want me to meddle in your love lives. Besides, she's barely twenty-one, I believe, much too young for you. Anyway, you've said it yourself, you're not interested in marriage."

He took a sip of his tea, wondering if he should be relieved or disappointed at his mother's comment. "All right, I suppose I could pick up Miss Fields the day after tomorrow."

The next morning while Peter was shopping for his weekly box of cigars, he recognized a long, thick braid pulled back in a messy bun at the nape of her neck—his sister-in-law, Imogene. She was holding her baby daughter, Daisy, and cooing to her while Daisy moved her little fingers in the air.

"You're a sight for sore eyes." Peter kissed Imogene on the cheek before picking up Daisy. "You haven't been to town in a while. I was about to send my deputies out to look for you two."

"You can blame this little one." Imogene pinched Daisy's cheek lovingly. "She has not let her father or me sleep for weeks."

Daisy gave both of them an innocent face. Peter quirked an eyebrow in Imogene's direction. "I only see an angel before me."

Imogene laughed. "She's only an angel for you and her father. We came to visit Penny and baby Colin. We just stopped by to get some sugar." She tilted her head to the side, where her husband was speaking to the town's blacksmith.

"How's Penny?" Peter gave a sympathetic nod. Men didn't discuss the nature of childbirth, but Derek had admitted Penelope's labor had been a hard one and she had lost a lot of blood. Thankfully, baby Colin had been born healthy. He hadn't had a chance to visit his other sister-in-law because she had been on strict bed rest, and it didn't seem proper.

"Much better." Imogene smiled. "Her cheeks are rosy again and Derek told us the midwife and the maid he hired are leaving this week. She misses you."

"I miss her too. I'll visit her next week, I promise." Peter shifted from foot to foot, feeling like a bashful schoolboy instead of a grown man nearing forty. Was it pathetic to ask Imogene for help in wooing a woman to be his bride? Perhaps he should ask Penelope. He shook his head. No, she was blunt, and she would probably spend the day giving him snarky replies. No, it would have to be Imogene. She had offered two years ago to get him to the altar.

"Is there something else?" Imogene asked kindly.

"Yes." He cleared his throat. "I thought… I believe it is time I look for a wife. I was hoping you would be able to assist in, just a suggestion, mind you, a proper woman. It seems more of your expertise after all."

Imogene's blue eyes flashed with joy as she squeezed his hand and squealed as if he had told her the Lord was coming to Sunday supper. "Oh, of course, I will help you! How exciting, Peter. Well, there is the kind widow, Mrs. Brown, though her husband did die only six months ago. She might not even be out of mourning yet, or there is Miss Paulette Crenshaw. I heard—"

"We'll discuss this later." Peter noticed Stefan was approaching his wife and daughter. "Not a word to anyone about this, Imogene. I mean it."

Imogene nodded like a proud soldier. Peter smiled. He knew he could count on her. If his brothers ever found out what he was doing, they would laugh in his face.

Bethany Fields was a rich city girl. Rich city girls did not leave New York for the middle of nowhere, Wisconsin. Rich city girls married before the age of twenty-one, and she was turning that age the day after tomorrow. Rich city girls did not give up a life of luxury to become a dowdy schoolteacher when she had barely passed school herself and hadn't dealt with a child under the age of twelve in years.

Yet here she was, in Redwood, Wisconsin. As she stepped out of the stagecoach, Bethany looked around.

She supposed as far as small towns went, it wasn't completely unfortunate looking. It was even kind of cute, like it belonged in a fairytale. Now, it only needed a princess. With her long, dark blonde hair, lovely green eyes, and cute button nose, she certainly looked like she could play the part of a princess. However, the unfortunate reality was she was as penniless as a poor pauper.

Her father, Edwin Fields II, had promptly cut her off the second she received her teaching certificate. By some divine intervention—well, plenty of her pin money at least—she had accepted a yearlong teaching job in rural Wisconsin. Mr. Fields had sworn she wouldn't last six months away from home and promised to dress her once again like a queen once she came to her senses.

Despite the obstacles her father had placed in her way, the endless pleading and the terribly long journey, Bethany had arrived in Wisconsin. If anyone had told Miss Fields a year ago she would be traveling to Wisconsin to become a schoolteacher, she would have laughed and practically made sure every worthwhile person in New York City shut their doors in their faces.

In fact, this hare-brained scheme had started just six month back, in her lavish bedroom in the townhouse she and her father shared, while her longtime nanny arranged her hair for a party instead of her clumsy lady's maid.

"Oh, my sweet, you are the loveliest rose in all of New York," Nanny whispered in her ear while Bethany shrugged her shoulders in fake modesty. She knew she was pretty. "If only your mother could see you now, she would die of shame and regret over the fact she chose lying with different men instead of becoming a respectable woman."

The comment had stopped her dead in her tracks. According to her father, her mother had died of childbed fever just mere days after giving birth to Bethany. Yet,

Nanny was acting as if Bethany's mother had purposely abandoned her and her father. No sane woman would, of course. Her father was rich and handsome. Bethany was the belle of the ball and had so many suitors, she didn't know which one to choose. She knew her nanny was advancing in age. She sometimes called her "Betty", a childhood nickname she hated, instead of her Christian name, but for some reason, this time Nanny sounded quite clear.

"What did you say, Nanny?"

Nanny didn't seem to notice the quivering in her voice or the shock on her face.

Could it be true? Bethany couldn't help but think as Nanny finished arranging fresh flowers in her hair. Her father hadn't mentioned her mother in years, and they'd never gone to visit her gravestone. Mr. Fields had said she had died when the young couple had been traveling and been buried somewhere else.

Bethany stared at the elderly woman who had raised her instead of her own mother. She didn't seem like she was lying or confused. But as she thought back to her own childhood, whenever she'd asked about her mother, her nanny didn't feed her the story her mother had died in childbirth; she simply didn't answer.

That night, Bethany didn't attend the party. Instead, she waited for her father to come home. When he did, she did everything she could to wrestle the truth from him. She cried, she screamed, she threatened a hunger strike like a spoiled child, until her father, who could never refuse her, finally broke down and told her the truth. Yes, Bethany was the product of a whirlwind romance with a young, beautiful prostitute, in a small town called Plentville, Wisconsin. Mr. Fields had begged the young prostitute named Ruth to marry him after she had the child. He told her his father would die soon, he would be the heir and Ruth could have everything if she just married him. Ruth said no. She didn't care about riches and wouldn't travel east. So, Edwin Fields II had baptized Bethany by himself and returned to New York, claiming to everyone that he had a short marriage during his travels, which had ended in his wife's death. No one had been the wiser. Not even Bethany.

Mr. Fields had hoped Bethany would soon forget the conversation and return to her usual shallow state of endless parties and appointments at the dressmaker. But something grew inside of Bethany. An obsession. She started wondering more and more about her mother, Ruth. Did she look like Bethany? Did Ruth also like the rain? Was she also terribly fond of chocolate? Was she still working as a lady of the night?

These were all the questions she wanted answers to, and unfortunately, her father didn't have much in terms of answers. Bethany had begged him for money to go to Plentville to see if her mother was there, but he had refused, saying Wisconsin was not a proper place for a gentle bred young lady. He said it was filled with cowboys, delinquents, and gunmen. Truth be told, cowboys and robbers sounded more interesting than plain New York.

Her father warned her if she insisted on going to Wisconsin, he would cut her off financially and she would not receive a penny. The idea of losing her money, shockingly, did not stop her. She wanted to see her mother badly and ask her why she had abandoned her. Not even the thought of never attending an elegant dinner party or never again wearing pretty slippers, was enough to stop her.

Bethany obtained a teaching certificate and later received a job offer to become a schoolteacher for the Redwood School. There was no open position in the school in Plentville and it was only a few hours away from Redwood. She was an excellent horsewoman, so she could ride to Plentville. Now, six months later, she was only hours away from her true destination.

"Have a good day, pretty lady."

The comment woke Bethany from her thoughts as the thin man with the two missing teeth who had driven the stagecoach waved goodbye at her. Bethany let out a silent huff. Who knew mid-western people had such bad manners?

Bethany grabbed her suitcase, nearly dragging it beside her. Perhaps, she shouldn't have packed the three extra pairs of shoes, the heavy winter coat, and the two silk shawls. From the letter she received from the head of the school board, she would be staying with the Meyer family and later on, boarding with the rest of her students' families. Truthfully, the idea of living in a new place every few weeks did not appeal to her, but beggars couldn't be choosers. With any luck, she would find her mother, convince her to come back to New York with her, and she would find herself back again in her goose feathers-filled bed before she knew it. Her father couldn't cut her off forever; she was his only heiress after all.

Miss Fields frowned, silently wishing she had come via train instead of a stagecoach, switching at the last minute. At least, on the train, she could get someone to help her with her bags, but riding on a train was so expensive. She was already low on funds as it was.

The Meyer family wouldn't be expecting her until tomorrow. She had arrived a day early after all, and it would be rude to show up unannounced. Besides, she didn't even know where they lived. A Mr. Ingalls was supposed to pick her up from the train station tomorrow.

No matter, she would have to dip into her nearly empty

satin drawstring purse and pay for an inn. Bethany found a cheap inn at the edge of town near the brothel named The Palace and the local saloon. The inn was run by an angry-looking man and his equally cross-looking wife. It was certainly not a decent place for Miss Fields to stay, but then again, in Wisconsin, no one knew who Edwin Fields II was.

The dingy little room she had paid for, for the night, was located at the end of a long, dark hallway that smelled like horses. When she pushed open the door of room nine, she frowned when she saw the plain room with the sad looking bed in the corner and dust bunnies on the floor. It was a far cry from the elegant bedroom she had left behind in New York, but it would have to do. There was no way she was going to go back to complain to the sour-looking couple. She was no longer in a position to argue.

Besides, it wouldn't kill her to do some light cleaning; even she knew how to sweep. Somewhat at least. Thankfully, there was a dustpan and a broom in the room. Bethany had barely gripped the broom handle when she heard noises coming from the paper-thin walls of the room next door.

It was the bubbly laughter of a woman, followed by a moan and then the low chuckle of a man. Bethany blushed as she realized what was going on next door. She might be a sheltered girl, but she wasn't a complete idiot. After all, servants talked more than they let on and she was perfectly aware of what happened between a man and a woman behind closed doors. She had never thought she would be expected to overhear.

Bethany hoped the moaning would stop, but it didn't. In fact, it seemed to grow even louder, and the woman had even started panting. She rested the end of the broom handle on her womanhood then started moving her hips slightly, causing the bundle of nerves between her legs to rub against the handle of the broom. The friction felt just heavenly. It made Bethany feel as if she were pushing a button that caused her instant happiness.

She moved the broom handle against her mound, almost desperately eager for more friction. She wanted more. She needed more. Bethany knew what she was doing was a nasty, sinful habit, but she hadn't done it in months. After the trip she'd had, she deserved some compensation. She gripped the handle and pushed it in almost slightly. Her damn dress was in the way.

Bethany concentrated on the man's deep rumbling. He sounded older. Manly. Handsome. Confident. By the way the woman was begging for him, he certainly seemed well informed on female pleasure.

"Oh, Peter," the woman murmured. "Please don't stop. I love having you lie on top of me. This allows me to feel your chest against my hands and I can stroke every muscle."

The man in question, whom she now knew was named Peter, slapped her. Or at least it sounded like flesh against a hardened palm, causing Bethany to awaken from her own activities. Much to her surprise, the woman didn't seem angry or shocked she had been slapped by the brute.

In fact, she only giggled and ordered, "More!" Which, quite frankly, caused Bethany to be quite confused.

Finally awake and once again properly ashamed on what she had done to pleasure herself, Bethany decided to put a stop to the moans and groans which were happening next door. She was getting up early after all, and she couldn't sleep properly if Peter and the laughing woman kept moaning and causing the bed to squeak at all hours.

She pushed the broom aside and smoothed down her dress, hiding all shameful remnants that she had just pleasured herself while the couple next door engaged in carnal desire. When she stood in front of the door, she raised her chin shrewdly like she had often done when addressing servants or people she disliked. She knocked on the door. No answer. She knocked again. Once again, no one opened the door.

When she was ignored again, Bethany lost her patience and pushed the door open. They were going to hear her one way or another. She froze in her steps. She hadn't heard noise in quite some time, so she'd believed they had been asleep or, at the very least, had put their clothes on. But she was very wrong indeed.

Both Peter and the unknown woman were still draped over the bed. The woman, a curvy redhead, didn't bother hiding her large breasts from Bethany's gaze. For a brief second, Bethany felt jealous. She wished her breasts looked as nice as hers instead of the handful she barely had. Her gaze traveled to the man draped over the redhead who looked more annoyed than embarrassed about being interrupted.

He was a large man, with a wide back and inky black hair. As the woman had mentioned, the muscles of his chest were clearly defined, and Bethany fought the urge to feel them as the woman had. His buttocks were firm and his thighs quite large. He was completely naked and didn't seem at all bothered that he was naked in front of two women.

He arched one dark eyebrow. It seemed he was almost laughing at her. What a scoundrel. He was not a gentleman. He was surely a man of ill repute. He was, as Bethany studied him, quite devilishly handsome.

"Yes?" his voice rumbled. Strong. Masculine. A voice that commanded respect and made Bethany shiver in her slippers.

Bethany stumbled a reply. She wasn't even sure if it was coherent because the redhead was staring at her as if she were an idiot. Bethany should have apologized or complained to the owners, but instead, she ran all the way back to her room like a coward.

Chapter 2

I f Peter were a real gentleman, he would have let the little chit squirrel away in her room without a second thought. However, the fact of the matter was that he was not a gentleman, and the prissy blonde was not getting away with barging into a stranger's room. Especially his room, which he had occupied for the sole reason of getting some much-needed pleasure from one of the lovely painted ladies from The Palace brothel next door.

Normally, clients were not allowed to take them from the brothel, but the madame trusted the sheriff and he always brought them home safe and sound, only a little weak in the knees and sore between their legs, but extremely content, nonetheless. The woman in his bed, Aubrey, was expensive and fun, but to be honest, thanks to the blonde's involvement, he didn't want to have sex anymore.

"Why are you even going there?" Aubrey twirled a piece of red, curly hair. They had spent enough time in each other's company to become old friends. Besides being great in bed, she was a good listener. The good thing about

The Palace was the women were sweet, charming, and clean, the complete opposite of the hellion who had just stomped inside who had been about to demand they be quiet.

Peter put on his trousers. Usually, an incident like this would have simply made him laugh and he would just continue on with his day, but strangely, the way this woman had entered the room bothered him. He wanted to give her a piece of his mind as he thought about her shrewish expression. Also, he was surprised he wanted to know her name.

"I just do." He put on his belt. "Someone needs to go over there and teach her it's not polite to pounce into a stranger's room. You can go, honey, we're done for the night."

Aubrey looked disappointed but nodded. Peter was even more irritated. He'd just lost a room, a woman, and half of his night, chasing after this foolish girl. He didn't recognize her, and as the sheriff, he knew everybody in Redwood. There hadn't been many newcomers lately, only a young family and a couple of bachelors.

Whoever this blonde was, she was here alone or with a female companion. No husband or father would allow a young woman to storm into a stranger's room unannounced unless they were weak-willed. He put on his shoes. That was another thing Peter hated, weak-willed men who would let their women run wild.

Peter exited the room and walked next door. He pounded on the door until he heard a feminine squeak. "Yes?"

"We need to talk." Peter tried to keep the famous Stevenson temper in check. He was dealing with a respectable young woman after all. "I'm the man from next door. We need to talk about the little stunt you just pulled. You ruined my night, darling."

"I don't know what you're talking about."

Peter chuckled as he rested his head against the door. "Feigning innocence is not going to help the situation, darling." Silence. "Do you know what I do with young women who fib? I whip their bottoms with my belt. I don't like liars, and you're much too pretty for fibs to be coming out of your mouth."

The woman let out a low gasp, and he bit his lower lip to keep from laughing. "I apologize if my companion and I were a bit loud, although it's rude to eavesdrop and even ruder to barge in without knocking."

"I did knock!" she snapped. "You were too preoccupied to answer."

Peter smiled; this interaction was much better. Not the scared little mouse act she was trying to pull. "I suppose we were a tad loud."

"Just a tad?"

He ignored her comment, mainly because even he knew it was inappropriate to continue this topic of conversation with a woman, let alone someone he didn't even know. "What's your name?"

"I'm tired. Go away, mister."

Peter stood there for a few minutes. There was little he could do unless he wanted his deputies to arrest him. "Good night then."

"Good night," the voice behind the door responded almost sweetly. "I'm sorry."

The next morning, Peter woke up feeling cranky. He was hungover, sexually frustrated, and his mother was driving him insane clucking about how Miss Fields was going to arrive on the ten a.m. stagecoach and he just had to go ahead to help her with her luggage. Apparently, Miss

Fields had sent a late letter to Mr. Ingalls, letting him know she would be arriving via stagecoach instead of the train. He left the house with his horses and the wagon a half an hour after nine, just to keep his mother from pestering him.

As Peter went down the familiar path to town, he wondered what kind of schoolteacher this Miss Fields would be. Most of the schoolteachers in Redwood were either young or old, dowdy or elegant, an old maid, or a woman eager to catch a husband. There usually was a new schoolteacher in the schoolhouse every couple of years since teachers were expected to quit once they married. The last one had married, so now he was stuck taking the horses and wagon to meet the new one.

Miss Fields would be staying with his parents for a year, and she and Peter would be living together for a couple of weeks until his house was finished. He might even give her a ride into town, since the schoolhouse was only a few feet away from the sheriff's office, even though it only took fifteen minutes to walk back to his parents' property.

The stagecoach station was nearly empty, with the exception of a young woman, in a fine pale blue dress, reading a book, wearing a fancy, matching hat. He stopped the horses as he stared at her, wondering where he had seen her. There were many petite blondes in town. When the young woman finally looked away from her book, Peter saw her face.

He recognized the judgmental green eyes, her pert little face, and her rosebud pink lips. It was the woman from last night, the one who had ruined his night. She was the schoolteacher? He looked around and noticed it was empty around her and his mother had been rather clear she was going to be there. This was going to be fun.

Once his gaze returned to hers, he almost laughed when Miss Bethany Fields' face turned pale white, then bright red. She grabbed her suitcase and started scurrying away like a field mouse across the station.

Peter gave an irritated sigh as he saw her move as far as her fancy shoes would let her. He got out of the wagon and practically ran toward her, wondering silently if it would be easier just to catch her, put her over his shoulder like a sack of rice, and take her back to his office to smack her bottom until she promised to behave.

"Miss Fields!" his voice boomed across the station, not caring who turned around to stare. It was her turn to be embarrassed. "Bethany, stop!"

"Oh, go away!" Bethany demanded, but she had stopped running, probably noticing that for each six steps she took, it only took Peter two to catch up. He was faster and was wearing thick boots instead of delicate shoes ordered from France or another European country. Even though she was dressed simply, even he could tell they were finely made clothes. Well, his mother had told him they were dealing with a city girl.

He murmured something under his breath as he hurried forward, gripped her wrist, and flipped her around as if she weighed nothing more than a piece of paper. Bethany's cheeks were flushed bright red, and her eyes seemed to sparkle with tears of embarrassment waiting to fall. "Have you gone selectively deaf? You're not listening. It seems you don't listen very well, Miss Fields. Perhaps that is a lesson I should teach you myself in the schoolhouse."

Bethany soon found her composure as she tried to pull away from Peter's iron tight grip, but he wasn't letting her go quite that easily. "You're not Mr. Harold Ingalls. He's supposed to pick me up. Your name is Peter. I heard that woman say your name last night. Or scream it if we're being accurate."

"Oh, so you were listening." He pursed his lips, enjoying the way she was squirming. He pulled her closer and placed a hand on the small of her back to keep her from fluttering around like a fish out of water. "Relax. I'm not going to hurt you. I'm Peter Stevenson and sheriff of this fine town. Mr. Ingalls is elderly, so I was asked to pick you up. You will be staying with my parents for the school year."

"I was supposed to stay with the Meyer family." She raised her pointed chin as if demanding obedience, but it only reminded Peter of a nervous kitten. "Not the Stevenson family."

"Mrs. Meyer left town. Her husband died a few weeks ago and it was decided you would be staying at my parents' house for the school year." He let go of the small of her back and she turned around as if asking why he dropped it from that particular spot. Peter chuckled; he was going to have fun with Miss Bethany this year. It was so easy to get under her skin. He returned his hand to her lower back. "My apologies, Miss Fields. I did not know you would miss my hand this much. Better?"

Bethany pinched his hand with her sharp nails. "Get your hands off a lady."

"I don't see a lady." Peter snorted as he picked up her heavy suitcase and placed it on the back part of the wagon. "I only see a peeping Tom. What is the female version of it, I wonder?"

"Stop." Bethany squinted her eyes shut. "Please."

Feeling pity for her, he stopped teasing her and instead helped her into the wagon. Peter whistled as they left town towards his parents' house. Bethany sat next to him, mainly looking at her lap. He almost felt disappointed when he saw her all meek and quiet. It was a known rule in Redwood that Peter Stevenson did not like unruly females, yet the blonde next to him was too quiet. He almost preferred when she was bratty and snarky. Like a true masochist, he decided to poke the bear.

"You weren't supposed to come to Redwood until today."

"My stagecoach got in early." Bethany fiddled with her thumbs. "I got a room at *that* inn because it was the cheapest one. Now, can we not talk about it, ever?"

"Honey, you got to see me in all my glory." He flashed her a smile and Bethany looked to the side, as if wondering if she should jump out of the wagon. "Do you know how many women would have wanted to be in that spot?"

"Well, I didn't want to be in that spot. Stop implying that I did!"

"If you didn't, then you wouldn't have barged in."

"I told you, sir, it was an accident."

"It didn't seem like an accident. It seemed you were throwing a hissy fit or, at the very least, having an outburst of some kind." Peter tipped his hat toward her. "Though I will admit, I was a tad bit loud with my lady companion, Miss Fields. Another thing, don't call me sir. Call me Peter. We are going to be living under the same roof, however temporary. There's no point in dealing with the formalities of it all."

Now, Bethany really did look like she wanted to jump out of the wagon. "What? You still live with your mother?"

Peter laughed. "Of course not. I'm staying at my parents' house temporarily while they finish construction on my own house. My mother and I will be the only ones at the house, though. My father is visiting his brother." Bethany grumbled something, probably contemplating her own misfortune. "Shall I call you Bethany? I like it better than Miss Fields."

"I guess," she grumbled, probably noting that Peter was

going to call her whatever he wanted. She looked around the wide, open fields. How long had she been in the wagon? Ten? Twenty minutes? "I never knew Redwood was going to be so pretty."

"We country mice get something right once or twice."

Bethany shifted in her seat, and Peter suddenly wondered how her bottom would look squirming over his lap. He imagined her lovely pale globes squirming under the hard administration of his palm. Peter scowled, scolding himself. This was not the time to get hard. Especially not for the new schoolteacher.

"Mr., I mean Peter. Would it be possible to forget about yesterday's incident? I'm mortified enough and I would rather not have this conversation again."

"We can forget about it. For now."

Before Bethany could ask him what he meant by that, a woman started screaming hello from a few feet away. She was standing on the porch of a pretty, two story house. "Who is that woman and why on earth is she screaming?"

Peter winced as he looked embarrassed. "She would be my mother. I apologize in advance for her assertiveness. My mother has been desperate for female companionship. My sisters-in-law have both given birth recently and they are indisposed. So, you will have to do."

Bethany ignored the jab. "Are you married?"

His lip curled into a smirk and Bethany almost regretted saying anything at all. "No. Why? Are you offering? You can be my little housewife."

Bethany raised her pert little nose in the air. "I wouldn't accept even if you would ask me."

"Good. You're too young for me. I'm thirty-eight."

"You look younger."

"Aw, thanks, hon."

She ignored his response. "Furthermore, I'm not too young. My birthday is tomorrow. I'm turning twenty-one."

Peter let out a low whistle. "Twenty-one is still awfully young. Though, perhaps you should be married instead of playing schoolteacher. What is a rich girl from New York doing in little Redwood, Wisconsin, anyway?"

Her cheeks were coated pink. "It's rude to talk about finances."

"Thankfully, I don't consider myself a perfect gentleman. That would be my brother, Derek."

"How did you know I was wealthy?"

"My mother," he answered simply as he stopped the wagon before hopping off to help her. "Not to mention, there are little things that give it away. Your clothes, the way you talk, your arrogance—"

"How dare you? You've known me for less than an hour!"

"Might I remind you about yesterday? You did barge in because you thought I was too loud. Here in Redwood, we don't do things because Miss Fields asks us to." Peter could see Bethany was getting upset and felt bad for pushing her. "I'm just wondering why someone who's wealthy would move to the country to teach."

"I like kids." Bethany flipped a blonde curl over her shoulder. "I plan to have some of my own. It's not any of your business why I decided to come to Redwood to teach. The school board should be grateful I came at all. I do have an excellent education after all. Now fetch my luggage; we mustn't keep your mother waiting."

"Yes, Miss Fields." Peter rolled his eyes as he helped her out of the wagon. They both walked towards the porch where Mrs. Stevenson practically suffocated Bethany with a tight hug. Bethany, however, took it much more gracefully than he had anticipated.

"Miss Fields, I'm delighted to meet you." Mrs. Stevenson finally released her from the hug. "I'm Bonnie Stevenson. You will be staying with me and my husband for the school year. He's away now, but he should be back in a few weeks. We are thrilled to have you here."

"Nice to meet you, Mrs. Stevenson. I'm Bethany Fields; please call me Bethany." Bethany fluttered her eyelashes sweetly. "Thank you for opening your home to me."

"Oh, it's no problem at all. We are thrilled to have you here, aren't we, Peter?"

"Ecstatic." His mother glared at him, and he pretended not to notice. "I'm going to put Bethany's suitcase in the guest bedroom."

After Bethany had settled into the guest bedroom, Mrs. Stevenson invited them for tea and cookies in the sitting room. Mrs. Stevenson had been talking nonstop while her new guest listened politely.

"We will provide anything you need, of course. We have household accounts in all of the stores in town, so anything you need, you can put it down on our tab. Or you can ask any of my sons if you need anything."

"We wish to serve you, Bethany." Peter took a sip of his tea and Bethany stomped her delicate slipper foot on his boot with much more force than he anticipated. Peter glared at her, and Bethany took an extra cookie in response.

"I know you will be busy with the children at the school." Mrs. Stevenson was completely oblivious about what was happening between Bethany and Peter. "I'll take care of the chores and the meals. Don't worry about a thing."

"Oh, no, Bonnie, I am more than happy to help with whatever you need."

"How sweet of you, dear."

Peter snorted. "I don't think she's being sweet, Mother. She probably can't actually do anything." He turned to her. "Have you ever actually cooked or used a broom before?"

Bethany's cheeks flushed red as she glared at him. "I have so! How do you know what I can or can't do?"

"Peter," his mother warned him, "you're being very rude."

He gave his mother a lazy smile. "I'm just teasing our Miss Fields. She shouldn't be so sensitive."

"Then you should keep your thoughtlessness to yourself," Bethany snapped.

Mrs. Stevenson gave a nervous chuckle as she stared at her son and then at her new guest. "Bethany, I planned a small dinner for you tonight, to welcome you. Nothing formal, just my two other more tolerable sons and their wives, along with my grandchildren, of course."

"How nice." Bethany had moved away from Peter and was now curled up on the side of the couch, nearly falling off. "I look forward to meeting them."

Peter's brothers, their wives, and their children arrived promptly at six in the evening. Much to his surprise, Bethany got along with them splendidly. Maybe his mother was right, and he had misjudged her. She wasn't a good cook, but she tried her best to help his mother and she doted on his niece Daisy and his nephew Colin. At the dinner table, she talked to his brother, Derek, who was a pastor, about an interesting article she'd read in a New York newspaper. She questioned Stefan, his other brother, a rancher, about his work with cattle, and she could make Imogene and Penelope laugh until they were red in the face. She was a good conversationalist and learning to be a good society hostess had obviously been one of the things she had learned back in New York.

Peter tried teasing her once or twice, but she always

responded sweetly in a way only he could detect her sarcasm, and it only made him look like a jerk. His mother had frowned at him so many times, it made him feel as if he were twelve years old. Derek and Penelope left before dessert because Penny was feeling exhausted and having a hard time keeping her eyes open.

After dessert, Bethany helped his mother clean up while he walked Stefan, Imogene, and baby Daisy back to their wagon.

"You like her," Imogene announced brightly, once they were out of earshot, as she held her sleeping daughter. "Bethany, I mean. It's quite obvious. It seems you don't need my help after all."

Peter tried his best not to flush red as he looked at his baby brother. "Control your wife, please."

"Why would I?" Stefan had a grin on his face, obviously enjoying having the upper hand for once. "She's right. You like Bethany; you kept teasing her all though dinner."

"Like when children tease their crushes at the schoolhouse."

"Exactly."

Peter opened his mouth to protest, but what could he say? He had been acting childishly, he must admit, but he didn't like Bethany. She was obviously a handful and much too young for him. Besides, he wanted someone older, demure, and sweet-tempered, the complete opposite of Bethany. "Both of you are insane."

"Oh, don't feel bad," Imogene assured him as her husband helped her up into the wagon. "I think it's adorable. I've seen you flirt, but I've never seen you head over heels in love with a woman before. It's cute. Well, it seems you don't need my help anymore."

"You haven't actually done anything. You're a terrible matchmaker."

Stefan looked confused at their discussion but didn't pry. No doubt he would ask his wife later on. Maybe it would be better if he did know, then all of the teasing would stop. Not that he couldn't take it, he simply thought it was annoying.

Imogene shrugged. "I'll keep looking if you want, but I think Bethany is perfect for you."

"She's too young for me," he repeated again.

"I'm younger than Stefan and so is Penelope with Derek. You don't see us complaining."

"Most of the time at least." Stefan kissed the back of Imogene's head, and she scoffed at him before pecking him on the lips. Peter watched them leave, wondering if they were even the teensiest bit right.

The next morning, Bethany sighed as soapy water splashed on her dress as she placed the breakfast dishes on the drying rack. Was she even doing this right? This was only the second time in her life she had washed dishes, and she was making a mess. However, she didn't want to seem like a burden to the sweet Mrs. Stevenson, and she wanted to prove to Peter that he was wrong and she could do simple household chores. The other two Stevenson brothers were so sweet, why did she have to get stuck living with the one she had seen naked and who took a special interest in teasing her nonstop?

She was alone in the house. Mrs. Stevenson had quickly departed into town when she found out it was Bethany's birthday today and had insisted she was going to bake her a cake. She hadn't seen Peter since last night.

Mrs. Stevenson told her he hardly ate breakfast and worked long hours. She just hoped she didn't have to see him frequently.

The front door opened, and she nearly jumped half a mile. She had never really lived by herself. Her old residence in New York was always bustling with activity or, at the very least, servants. Her jumping heart settled when she realized it was just Peter. He was dressed in all black and she saw his shiny sheriff's badge.

"Good morning," Peter greeted her as he looked at her apron. "Aren't we looking domestic? Happy Birthday by the way."

"Thank you." She cleared her throat. "Do you want some breakfast? I could try to scramble some eggs."

"No, I don't eat breakfast." He was unusually serious today. "I saw my mother in town. She was talking with Mrs. Randall; she'll probably be talking with her for at least an hour."

"She went into town to buy the ingredients for a birthday cake."

"That's nice of her. You probably won't be sitting tonight when you cut your cake."

"Excuse me?" Bethany felt her cheeks grow pink. "What is that supposed to mean?"

"That is why I came back. There are some things we need to take care of, which I assume you don't want me to take care of in front of my mother." Peter didn't explain right away as he gripped her wrist and practically dragged her back to her bedroom. She tried pulling away but was quite unsuccessful as he was much too strong. Once they were back in her bedroom, he closed the door behind himself.

Bethany rubbed her wrist as she turned to glare at him. "Would you mind explaining why we're here?"

"Because you're getting a spanking." He said the words so matter of factly that, at first, all Bethany did was laugh, but when he wasn't laughing in return, she quickly sobered up.

"What?" she screeched as she looked around the room wondering if there was something she could do to knock him down. "You can't spank me! Why?"

"To teach you that you shouldn't barge into a stranger's room," Peter explained calmly as he sat on the bed on her flowered quilt. He was holding her heavy hairbrush from her vanity. "You were lucky it was just me, but it could have been a dangerous situation. There are dangerous people out there, Bethany, and believe it or not, there are some people who do not think your outbursts are particularly cute."

"It wasn't an outburst!" she protested, even though, technically, it had been.

"Outburst, temper tantrum, whatever you want to call it." He tapped the back of the hairbrush against his thigh. "It was still dangerous. What if it had been a man who was doing something in that room no one was supposed to find out about? You could have easily been killed for just opening the door."

"But it wasn't a strange man." Bethany was starting to panic, noticing for once that Peter was quite serious. "It was just you and your woman friend. I made a mistake. I don't deserve to get spanked."

Peter chuckled. "Honey, women don't have a say on when they get spanked. Otherwise, no discipline would happen. I don't consider myself a lenient man. I wouldn't be a very good sheriff if I was. If you had barged in by accident, I would accept it, but you barged in because things weren't occurring like you expected them to. Now, be a good girl and get over my lap."

Bethany hesitated as she wondered what she should do. Cry? Complain to Mrs. Stevenson? Call the sheriff; wait, he *was* the sheriff. "You can't spank me! You're not my father or my husband."

"Maybe, but you are living under my roof, which means I'm responsible for you."

"Your mother's roof. Does she know you're planning on beating me a day after my arrival?"

"I'm not beating you; I'm spanking you. I came because I knew she would be gone, and I wanted to give you some privacy. You could tell her the entire story if you want. I won't be the one who's embarrassed." When he saw her hesitating, he patted his knee. "Get over my lap, Bethany, don't make me come get you."

Much to her surprise, Bethany found her feet moving. She hesitated when she stood in front of him, and Peter gently placed a hand on her lower back and lowered her over his lap. She could feel his thick knee pressing against her belly. Bethany wanted to burst into tears. She knew what she had done had been foolish, but foolish enough that she had to be spanked for it?

"Good girl. I will spank you over your dress, to preserve your modesty." He started rubbing her bottom, causing a shiver to run down her spine. Her rump had never been touched before and it felt odd feeling his thick fingers over her clothed bottom. Her belly also felt warm as she concentrated on how his hand felt over her skirt. Strong. Heavy. Masculine.

"How generous," she snapped.

"It is generous." Peter chuckled as he started rubbing the back of the hairbrush against her rump. "A proper spanking is always conducted bare bottomed. You'd better pray you never find yourself in this situation again, Miss Fields, I don't like repeating myself."

Bethany opened her mouth to argue, but nothing came out, even though a thousand insults were at the tip of her tongue. However, she was not quiet for long, as a screech escaped from her lips three seconds later.

Peter had raised the brush high in the air before landing it in the middle of her cheeks with a hard swat. Bethany didn't scream after the one screech, didn't cry, just held her breath as she felt her entire body shift forward from the strength of the swat.

She couldn't believe he was actually going through with it. Worse, she couldn't believe she had been stupid enough to agree. Yes, she had barged in unannounced and, yes, it had been rude, but Peter was still a complete stranger.

A second smack landed on the back of her thighs, and she whimpered. The second swat was somehow worse than the first one. She wasn't sure if the spanking hurt or if she was simply feeling humiliated. She had never been spanked before and wasn't sure what the appropriate number of swats were for a first spanking.

"I hope you think twice before barging in on strangers," Peter announced coolly as he gripped her hairbrush tightly in his hand while it continued to fall crisply. Even through her heavy dress and petticoats, Bethany still felt every time the heavy brush landed on her rear. "I have no problem repeating this lesson again, young lady, if you disobey. Will we have to have this conversation again in the future?"

"No!" she practically screamed at him, her teeth on edge. The hairbrush was falling faster and harder now, and he was paying special attention to her sit spots and the fleshiest part of her cheeks. As soon as it began, the brush stopped falling.

Peter immediately scooped her up in his arms and stood her up, so she was facing him before he pulled her in for a hug. She blinked her green eyes in confusion. "It's over?" Yes, her bottom was feeling a bit tender, and her eyes stung a bit, but she wasn't full-on crying like she had thought she was going to be.

"You were expecting more?" he smirked. "I could give you more if you want. Though, I thought I would be gentle with your first spanking. Think of it as a birthday spanking, sweetheart. Nothing too harsh, but it gives you a taste of what you should expect if you cause me any trouble." He tipped her chin forward, "Are you planning on being naughty?"

"No." Bethany's cheeks felt hot and sweaty. What was wrong with this man and why was he making her feel like this?

"Bethany!" Mrs. Stevenson called out from downstairs, saving her from an awkward conversation. "I'm back."

Peter winked. "Someone is looking for you, birthday girl."

Chapter 3

"How long are you planning to pout?" Peter grinned at Bethany. Although she was sitting right next to him on the wagon, she'd scooted as far away from him as she could. He was surprised she hadn't tumbled over.

Bethany had been giving him the silent treatment ever since he spanked her yesterday, which he had been expecting. It was clear, a spoiled, rich girl like her wasn't used to getting a spanking, though she would have been better off if she had. Her birthday had been a delightful affair, even though he had to admit that it hurt she'd talked to every family member but him. He was surprised she hadn't smashed his slice of birthday cake on his face.

As they approached the one room schoolhouse, Peter noticed there were a few children waiting for her, carrying tin pails with their lunches inside and holding books to their chests. Peter turned around to face her. "I will pick you up at three o'clock to take you back to Mother's, and if it wasn't obvious, I will deliver you to the schoolhouse safe and sound in the mornings."

Bethany scowled at him like an angry cat. "That is hardly necessary. I am more than capable of walking."

"Miss Fields, if you are going to be a teacher, you definitely have to act a bit more grown up." Peter used his thumb and index finger to tilt her chin forward. "I know you are more than capable of walking, but I would have more peace of mind if I knew where you were."

"What if I want to go shopping after school?"

"Then you can; you can just drop by my office when you're done, but you need to tell me beforehand where you're running off to. Understood?" He raised a dark eyebrow, and she let out an adorable blush, no doubt thinking that if she disobeyed him, she was going to end up over his knee again. Good. The little chit needed the discipline, and whichever poor fool she married would thank him.

He stopped the wagon in front of the schoolhouse. "Thank you for the ride," she replied primly as she got out of the wagon. "I will see you at three o'clock."

"Hold on, Bethany, let me give you a piece of advice."

"Yes?"

"Be firm."

"What?" She looked confused.

"These kids. Your students, they are not the proper misters and misses you're used to. They might be children, but some of them can be quite naughty. Don't be afraid to be strict when you need to be, or they will never take you seriously."

"I know how to handle a classroom," she replied coldly as she took her small bag which contained a shawl and a sandwich Mrs. Stevenson had lovingly made for her. "Besides, I passed my examinations."

Before Peter could offer any other explanation, she

hurried inside the schoolhouse like a scared deer. She was definitely the oddest schoolmarm he had ever encountered.

Bethany stood by the window, peeking through the beige lace curtains in the schoolhouse, watching as Peter left. How dare he think she wouldn't be able to handle classroom. Why, she had organized balls and charities for a hundred people. Surely, she could handle a couple of unruly children.

Once Peter had left, she looked around the schoolhouse. It was a small room, with a fireplace for the winter months. It had a large chalkboard, twelve desks, a teacher's desk which contained a Bible, a primer, a first reader, an arithmetic book, and a history book. There was also a large ruler on the desk that Bethany decided to put away for now. On her desk, there was also a roster with the names of the students she would be expected to teach.

Mrs. Stevenson had warned her last night during dinner that in the country, most boys stopped attending school by the age of fifteen, either to help at their family's farm, to work, or to learn a trade. Many families lived too far from town or were too busy to send their children to school. She would mostly be teaching little boys and girls and a couple of older girls. As her green eyes went through the roster, she counted six girls and five boys. Three of the girls were six, one girl was ten, and the last girl was twelve. There were four eight-year-old boys and one six-year-old boy. Overall, it was a small classroom which, God willing, would make the transition easier.

Bethany sighed, wondering for the one hundredth time since she arrived in Redwood if this had been the smartest thing to do. She hadn't even liked school when she attended her prestigious all-girls private academy and now, she was expected to teach it.

There was a shy knock on the door as a slightly older girl peeked in. "Good morning, miss, is it time for school?"

She looked at the clock and noticed it was five minutes past eight o'clock in the morning. Drat, she had forgotten to ring her bell. She snatched the small bell on her desk and started ringing it. "Thank you for reminding me, uh—"

"Beatrice," Beatrice offered. "I'm twelve years old. My sister Susie is six."

"Thank you for reminding me, dear." Bethany felt frazzled. "You can go sit down; let me get everyone."

Unfortunately for Bethany, the only moment of peace she knew were the first, few precious moments when she was jotting down names of her students for her roster. After that, there was one disaster after another. She couldn't get the class to quiet down, she didn't know how to quite explain the difference between "they're" and "their", and when she was trying to help little Susie with an arithmetic problem that was taking both of them fifteen minutes to solve instead of five, another mishap occurred. Little Bobby, who was quicky turning into her enemy even as an eight-year-old, had managed to cover the green skirt of her dress with black ink.

Bethany looked longingly at the delicate material made by the finest dressmaker in New York, knowing it was beyond ruined. She was too upset and too crabby to yell at him. Her green eyes stared desperately at the clock. Only ten more minutes until three o'clock, then she would be free. Surely, they could behave for three minutes.

She went wearily to her chair. The only time she had

sat down today, was to inhale the sandwich Mrs. Stevenson had prepared. Bethany pulled out her chair from her desk, looked at the seat of the chair, and let out a scream.

Peter looked at his pocket watch and saw it was five minutes until three o'clock. He would pick her up and drop her off at the house before he returned to the office for the rest of the afternoon. Suddenly, he heard a shriek coming from the schoolhouse. *Bethany.*

He rushed inside and saw her hollering her head off while looking at a frog jumping up and down all over her desk. Some of the students were laughing, while others looked on in pity and guilt. It was clear, some mischievous student or two had pulled off a prank and by the look on Bethany's skirt, it wasn't the first time.

Peter pursed his lips and quickly grabbed the frog in his hand. He then turned to the students, who immediately sobered up when they saw the sheriff. "Who did this?" he demanded, raising the frog in the air. "Who thought it would be fun to prank Miss Fields?"

No one responded, and Bethany had finally stopped screaming to stare silently, her cheeks pink. Not wanting to embarrass her any further, he looked at the rest of the class sternly. "The behavior you have shown Miss Fields is abhorrent, and should it happen again, I shall inform each of your parents with no hesitation. Is that understood?"

The children meekly nodded before Bethany weakly told them they could go. They scurried off like scared mice. Peter turned to her, obviously feeling pity for her as he gruffly asked, "Are you all right?"

Bethany nodded, barely daring to look at him. Peter

hoped she wouldn't cry. He was helpless when it came to crying females unless they were over his knee or they were cries of pleasure.

"I'm going to release this outside," he finished awkwardly. "Come outside when you get your stuff."

Ten minutes later, they were on their way back to the Stevenson house. Peter wanted to comfort her, but he wasn't quite sure what to say. "You're unusually quiet. Tough first day?"

As soon as he said those words, the waterworks started, and Peter almost wished he hadn't said anything. "Oh, Peter, it was horrible!" she blubbered as she struggled to speak. "I am horrible at teaching, which, of course, I would be since I hated school and I've never wanted to be a teacher."

Between her tears, he threw her a puzzled look. "Then why did you apply to be a teacher?"

For a second, Bethany stopped crying to stare at him. She hesitated for a moment before she said, "I just wanted to leave New York. Now, it seems I have gotten myself into a terrible mess. I don't know how I will be able to survive the school year."

"Listen, honey, don't let the kids rile you up," he mused. "They will try to test you. Especially the little ones. Don't hesitate to use me as a threat whenever they are riling you up."

Neither of them said anything on the short ride back to the elder Stevenson's' property. Every once in a while, Bethany sniffled, and Peter looked at her with concern. He wasn't good with tears, especially when they belonged to a woman. He had grown up with mostly men, and the women he did spend time with, rarely cried in his company.

He stopped the wagon in front of the house, pulled out

his handkerchief and placed it on her nose. "Blow," he instructed firmly. "I can't send you inside. My mother will throw a fit if she thinks I made you cry."

Bethany rolled her eyes but did as she was told. The both of them walked awkwardly toward the house. "You don't have to stay a teacher forever," he said. "You can quit."

"And do what?" she scoffed. "I've already been disinherited. I don't have a single penny to my name, Peter, in case you've forgotten."

Peter didn't say anything and instead, he just opened the door. Much to their surprise, he found his mother hastily dragging a traveling suitcase. "Good, you're here. I need you to take me to the train station. How was your first day, Bethany dear?"

Bethany offered a wry smile in response. "Are you going on a trip, Mrs. Stevenson?"

"And what's the hurry?" Peter demanded. His mother wasn't usually a person who did things without notice or hastily.

"Unfortunately, I am." Mrs. Stevenson turned to Peter. "Your father fell off his horse and broke two of his ribs. I need to leave Redwood immediately and go to him."

Peter looked at her, perplexed. "What?"

Mrs. Stevenson nodded, obviously annoyed. "Your father and uncle decided to act like a couple of idiots and ride their horses intoxicated. Pardon the language, dear. Your father couldn't handle the reins. I just received a telegram, and your uncle broke his leg when he fell off the horse. They need someone to take care of them, so I am making the journey myself."

"No, you won't," Peter blurted out. "I'll come with you. It's dangerous for a female to travel alone."

"You're the sheriff," she chided him gently. "You can't

leave for a few weeks, and Derek is a pastor, and Stefan is a rancher. You are grown men with responsibilities, not to mention your brothers have wives and babies to look after. Your brothers know of my decision, and they have made their peace with it."

"Mother—"

"Peter," she mocked his tone of voice. "I am perfectly capable of traveling. Your uncle does not live very far away, and I will mostly be housebound. I will be back in a month or so with your father in tow, once he and your uncle have healed." Mrs. Stevenson turned to Bethany, who had been politely pretending not to overhear the conversation. "Of course, that leaves you, my dear, in quite a predicament. I won't be able to serve as your host if I'm not here. Perhaps you could move in with Derek and Penelope while I'm away. Stefan and Imogene live too far."

"She can continue staying here," Peter blurted out. The idea of seeing Bethany only in passing and at church on Sunday irked him. He wanted to see her more than only a few brief meetings every week. "My house is still not finished, and Derek and Penelope are still adjusting to baby Colin."

Bethany spoke up. "It isn't proper for me to stay in the house with an unmarried man."

"I'm the sheriff," he scoffed, as if that solved everything. "Your virtue is more than safe with me."

Bethany opened her mouth to respond, but then she pinkened, obviously remembering her previous spanking. Instead, she looked down at her shoes.

If Mrs. Stevenson noticed the awkwardness between them, she didn't say anything. "You are the sheriff, and it is a family emergency. I could have Penelope or Imogene stop by every couple of days just to check in. Would that make things better, dear? If that makes you uncomfortable, I'm sure we can make other arrangements."

Peter glared at his mother.

Bethany looked up. "That won't be necessary, Mrs. Stevenson. I'll stay here."

Chapter 4

A couple of days later, after Mrs. Stevenson had left, Bethany told Peter she would wait for him until he was done with his work for the day instead of having him take her home to an empty house like he usually did. She had told him she wanted to spend some time with his sister-in-law, Penelope Stevenson. That was true, but she also wanted to get some recipes from her. Ever since Mrs. Stevenson had left, she and Peter had been living off restaurant food since neither of them were good cooks. Having grown up with servants, cooks, and nannies, Bethany was lucky she knew how to make tea.

They couldn't live off restaurant food until Mrs. Stevenson came back, and Bethany felt she had to make some effort, especially since Peter was taking her to and from work and taking care of whatever she needed. Ever since the sheriff had stopped by, the children were behaving better. However, she was still a terrible teacher despite earning her teaching certificate, but she would worry about that later. After all, it wasn't the reason she had come to Wisconsin.

"You're right on time," Penelope greeted her as she opened the door. "I made tea and I just put the baby down. Derek is at the church, so it's just us girls. We'll have plenty of time to talk."

"Actually, I was hoping we could do more than talk," the blonde admitted shyly. "Mrs. Stevenson will be gone for a while, and Peter and I can't live off restaurant food forever. I was wondering if you can give me a recipe or two that even a hopeless cook like me can do. Peter will come pick me up in an hour."

"Of course." Penelope shot her a curious look. "Does Peter know you're asking for cooking tips?"

"No," she scoffed. "He'll just tease me like he always does."

"That is true, Peter does love to tease."

In the next hour, Penelope wrote the recipe for buttermilk pancakes, vegetable soup, mashed potatoes, fried chicken, and apple pie on five, small, blank cards. Bethany looked at the cards helplessly, wondering if she would be able to do this without burning down the Stevenson kitchen. "Thank you for doing this. You must think me a complete fool for not being able to cook a decent meal."

"Of course not," Penelope replied kindly. "We are all good at different things, and everyone needs help every once in a while. Now, you'd better hurry before Peter storms in demanding to know what's taking so long. Good luck."

Bethany thanked her again as she hurried to the wagon where Peter was waiting impatiently. "What took you so long?"

"Oh, you know how it is when women get to talking. Don't be so nosy."

Peter snorted.

The next afternoon, Bethany was trying to hastily cook

dinner after Peter had dropped her off. She was trying to make a simple dinner of fried chicken and mashed pota- toes. The key word was trying. She frowned as she looked at the chicken. Was it supposed to look this dark? Maybe it would make it a bit crispier.

"Oh, damn!" she swore as she finished stirring the mashed potatoes. For some reason, they kept sticking to the pan. Bethany looked around the kitchen and couldn't believe the mess she had made in such a short time. It would take forever to clean it up. How did Mrs. Stevenson, Penny, and Imogene manage to cook so effortlessly?

An hour later, Peter arrived, and he quickly looked over her shoulder where she was trying to see if the chicken was edible or not. He rested his chin on her shoulder. "How on earth did you manage to ruin fried chicken, woman?"

Bethany's cheeks turned pink. "I didn't ruin it; it's just a little different."

"It looks burnt."

She scowled at him as she felt her cheeks turn cran- berry red. Nobody laughed at Bethany Fields. She didn't care if she *was* living in his mother's house. She was nobody's laughingstock. "If you think my cooking is so horrible, you don't have to eat it!"

Bethany turned around, hitting him straight in the jaw with her thick blonde hair pulled back in a ponytail.

Peter rubbed his jaw. "Oh, come on, Beth, it was a joke. No need to get your feathers all ruffled."

"Well, it wasn't a very funny joke!"

"Beth—"

"Oh, leave me alone!" Before he could say anything else that sounded remotely stupid, Bethany stomped upstairs. She regretted attempting anything for that awful man. Thankfully, he didn't attempt to chase after her, or she would have gladly thrown him down the stairs.

She decided to take a bath and then get into bed. The tub was already prefilled in the washroom with cold water, which she preferred. Thankfully, it was still warm enough that she could take cold baths without catching a cold.

Bethany closed the door to the washroom, knowing even Peter would have the decency not to just storm in. She took off her clothes and got into the bath, quickly submerging her body into the water. She rested her head on the back of the tub.

Stupid Peter, she thought bitterly, *and after I tried so hard to make it taste good. He could have at least tried it before he laughed at it.*

She wallowed in self-pity for fifteen minutes before she decided to get out of the tub. She stepped out and reached for the fluffy towel she had placed on the nearby table. A pair of watery brown eyes stared back at her. A field mouse.

Bethany let out a scream as she forgot about the towel and let it fall to the floor. She raced out of the bathroom, half forgetting she was naked. Her only goal was to get away from the mouse.

At the same time, Peter rushed up the stairs, obviously alarmed by her screams. Before he could even say anything, Bethany ran into him, knocking him down.

Her breasts were crushed against his hard chest and his hands almost instantly rested on her waist. Bethany blushed as she squirmed, knowing very well, she was fully naked on top of a man who was not, and would never be, her husband. She wanted to die of embarrassment.

"I'm s-sorry," she stammered as she tried to raise herself up, but then she pushed herself down when she realized she didn't want him to see her full breasts. "There was a mouse on top of a towel. It scared me and I..." Bethany didn't continue; she just looked at how Peter was staring at her. His hazel eyes were staring instantly at her flushed face. His warm hands were on her back and slowly going down to rest on her hips. Before she could even ask why he was staring at her so intently, he did something shocking.

He lifted her head and pulled her in for a kiss.

Chapter 5

Bethany was grateful that the next day was Saturday and there was no school. By the time she crawled out of bed, it was almost ten and Peter had left for work hours ago. As she sipped on her tea, her mind continued going back to the terrible night before.

She squeezed her eyes shut. How was it possible that the same obnoxious man had spanked, seen her naked, and kissed her, all in the span of less than a month? After he had kissed her yesterday, he had apologized almost instantly before closing his eyes, helping her up, and allowing her to scurry back into her guest room to keep the shred of dignity she had left.

The last thing he had said to her last night, had been through closed doors, letting her know he had gotten rid of the mouse and that it must have crawled in from the window. No mention of the kiss. He had left early this morning for work, and she didn't know if she should be grateful or annoyed.

The kiss. Oh, that kiss. Bethany had been kissed before, but never like that. The kiss had been short and sweet, but in that short span, Peter had made her feel something no other man had made her feel. Passion. Desire. Need. All roped into one.

Her body had quivered as she rested it on top of him, her breasts crushed against his rock-hard chest, as her hips seemed to sink even further. He made her feel—

Her thoughts were rudely interrupted when she heard a knock on the door. It was Stefan Stevenson, the youngest Stevenson brother. She opened the door and forced a smile on her face. She wondered if Peter had said anything to his brother. If he had, she would kill him.

Bethany bit her tongue. She needed to stop thinking about Peter and his kiss. The only reason she had come to this little town in the middle of nowhere, was to look for her mother, not daydream. She had a mission to complete.

She opened the door and plastered a fake smile on her face. Stefan was holding a small basket and she could smell the cinnamon bread as soon as she opened the door. Penelope and Imogene knew Bethany was terrible in the kitchen and they had made it their personal mission to make sure she and Peter were fed. She wondered how they managed to do it all. She could barely make tea and both of them had husbands and a baby to look after.

"From Imogene, cinnamon bread." Stefan peeked around. "Is Pete here?"

"No, he's at work." Bethany quickly grabbed the basket, eager to steer the conversation away from Peter. "Actually, since you're here, how far is a town called Plentville?"

Stefan raised a dark brow. "About two hours by horse. Willow Oak is the closest town to Redwood, only an hour away. Honestly, all you have to do is continue riding east and you'll find it quite easily. Are you itching to buy something, perhaps a new hat?"

"Perhaps," Bethany replied noncommittally. Two hours wasn't far away, but she would have to go over the weekend unless she faked illness in order to miss work. She frowned, but over the weekend, she was sure she would have Peter sniffing around and that was what she wanted to avoid.

"I'm sure Peter could take you one of these days, or maybe I can. Imogene has never been there, and we could take the baby and make a day trip out of it."

"Oh, no, both of you are far too busy," she said sweetly, being as charming as she possibly could. "I noticed Mr. Stevenson has two horses. I am an expert horse rider myself; you see, I have taken lessons since I was a child and—"

"No," Stefan interrupted her, sounding harsher than she had ever heard him before. "It's not safe. Wisconsin is not New York. Most towns are civilized, but there are still some rough areas. A young woman traveling two hours away without a chaperone is asking for trouble. I'm sure whatever the reason you have for visiting Plentville is not worth more than your life. I'll speak to Peter, and we'll come to an arrangement."

She bit her tongue to prevent herself from scowling. After a few more minutes of mindless chatter, Stefan excused himself and Bethany closed the door. She couldn't wait for days until Stefan or Peter might be able to give her a ride. Besides, she wouldn't be able to question the townspeople to see if they knew her mother without Imogene or one of the Stevenson brothers wondering what she was doing.

No, she had to do this now. The clock on the wall marked twelve o'clock. If she went to Plentville now, she could arrive by two, spend an hour there, and be back at Redwood by five o'clock. Peter wouldn't come home until dinnertime, and neither Imogene nor Penelope had plans to visit her today.

A smile curled on her lips. It was almost too perfect. Stefan had mentioned it was rather easy to get to, even if it was farther away than she had expected. Within minutes, she was out of the house and heading toward the small stables on the back of the property.

Since Stefan had taken over the family cattle ranch, the elder Mr. and Mrs. Stevenson kept only two horses on the property. After struggling with saddling the mare—she had never had to saddle her own horse after all—she was on her way.

"Please," she said a silent prayer, "let me find my mother."

Peter usually ate lunch at his office or at a restaurant in town if he had been too lazy to make his own lunch. However, his second in command, Deputy Clarkson, had noticed him fidgeting all morning and finally told him to take a walk.

So, he ended up at his parents' house in search of Bethany. He needed to apologize to her, even though it had been neither of their faults. Just a terrible, embarrassing occurrence, nothing more.

He could feel himself growing rock hard whenever he thought about her soft breasts pressing against his chest. He had wanted to fondle and kiss them so badly. Every part of her was soft, and when his calloused hands touched the small of her back, he wanted nothing more than to make love to her even though he knew how terribly improper it was.

Bethany was a high society lady, the schoolteacher,

though a terrible one at that, not to mention, an unmarried young woman in his parents' house who was, of course, very young for him. He would apologize, and then he would work on courting and marrying someone more age-appropriate and not someone so sheltered, naïve, and so... adorable.

He sighed as he walked toward his parents' house. What was it about Bethany that made him not stop thinking about her? Usually, someone as spoiled and headstrong would irritate him, but he found it oddly cute, even though she definitely needed a spanking to straighten her out once in a while.

"Beth?" he called out as he entered the surprisingly silent house. "Bethany?"

For a second, he thought she was childishly ignoring him, but the more he called out to her and received no response, the more worried he felt. He checked all of the rooms, but she was nowhere to be seen. Then he went to the small stables in the back and noticed the mare was missing.

Panic immediately set in. Where was she? Was she hurt? Could she even ride? When he got ahold of her, he was going to give her a stern talking to. Preferably with her over his lap. He knew she was not with his sister-in-law Penny, because he had waved hello to her on the way over and she had been by herself with her baby.

The next person in mind was Imogene; his sister-in-law didn't ride so Bethany must have gone to visit her. She didn't have many other friends. The blonde was usually pretty good at keeping him up to date with her whereabouts, but her feathers were ruffled enough to act a bit rebellious.

Letting out curse words under his breath, he headed to his brother's ranch. He found Imogene cooking dinner and after answering his endless questions, she admitted she hadn't heard from the schoolteacher.

"Stefan said this morning she wanted to go to Plentville," Imogene mused. "He thought we could make a day trip out of it. Won't that be nice?

"Plentville?" Peter sounded distracted. Plentville was smaller than Redwood and hosted a rougher crowd. There was no way Bethany was interested in going there. "Sure, nice. Listen, Imogene, I have to go."

"Don't worry." Imogene looked at him with sympathy. "I'm sure Bethany is all right. She is quite resilient."

"Believe me," Peter groaned as he headed outside. "Resilient isn't quite the word I would use."

Either Stefan gave terrible directions, or Bethany had been a little too optimistic about this entire journey, but she ended up getting lost. Thankfully, she ended up running into a stagecoach and the driver gave her more clear directions. She finally arrived in Plentville at noon and believed if she left by one, she would still be able to return to Redwood by dinnertime and no one would be the wiser.

She wished she knew her mother's maiden name, but her father had only mentioned her as Ruth. The brothel was probably the best place to start, though she doubted her mother was still a painted lady.

Still, the idea of entering a brothel made her embarrassed and would probably not be the best plan, given her situation. Surely, there were other people in town who knew her mother.

Bethany went to the apothecary, the post office, the general store, three restaurants, the lumber mill, the church, even the local schoolhouse, but no one seemed to have heard of a woman named Ruth.

By two o'clock, she was exhausted and nearly dragging her feet. She desperately wanted to sit down with a cool glass of lemonade, but she knew she needed to head back. She knew perfectly well if she wasn't there by dinnertime, Peter would have her head.

Anyone with half a brain would have probably called it quits. After all, her parents had met nearly twenty-two years ago. For all she knew, Ruth was dead, had moved away, or maybe she had even changed her identity, but if there was one thing Bethany had, it was pure stubbornness.

Like a dog with a bone, she couldn't leave the idea of her mother alone. She had to find her or at least make sure she really was no longer in Plentville. If she had truly moved on, then she would hire a private investigator or she would force her father to hire one.

Bethany sighed as she rode back to Redwood. She would have to go back to Plentville sometime, which meant more sneaking around. While she wasn't usually squeamish about breaking the rules, she felt uncomfortable breaking Peter's rules. More than likely because he wasn't one to let things slide.

Chapter 6

Bethany arrived at half past four, almost two hours before Peter was due to return. She thanked her lucky stars as she put the exhausted mare back into the stable after giving her some well-deserved water.

She was practically skipping, giddy at her good fortune as she went inside the house. Her giddiness quickly stopped when she entered the house and noticed a very angry sheriff staring back at her, reminding her of a raging bull.

His large arms were crossed over his chest, his hazel eyes were narrowed at her, and steam was practically coming out of his ears and nose. If Bethany hadn't been so nervous, she would have burst out laughing.

"Hello," she greeted him primly, refusing to be nervous. Somehow, facing him when he was angry, was worse than facing him after he had seen her naked and had kissed her. "You're awfully early, aren't you? I haven't even gotten dinner started."

"And you're awfully late, miss."

"I was out."

"For four hours?"

The remark caused her to stiffen as she slowly turned around. "How l-long h-have you—"

"Long enough," he interrupted, obviously enjoying her stammering. Bethany looked at the wooden spoon in his hand, and she gulped. She had personally never been spanked with the implement, but the children of the house servants had definitely felt the spoon on their behinds. "Now, I am going to ask you again, where were you? Don't lie."

"I went to Plentville," she replied shakily.

"Why?"

"I-I can't tell you."

Peter took a deep breath, obviously frustrated. "Why not?"

"It's sort of a private matter. It's nothing bad, I swear it."

"Ladies shouldn't swear." He placed one hand on his hip while his other still held the dreaded wooden spoon. "We won't get into it now. Now, young lady, march upstairs unless you want to get your bottom whacked in my mother's sitting room."

"You can't spank me!" she protested. If she was trying to sound like a mature woman, she was failing, especially since she sounded like a spoiled child instead, which she supposed she was. "I'm a guest in your home."

"A guest who doesn't seem to care about her own safety," he corrected darkly. "Bethany, what you did was very dangerous. You could have gotten killed, or worse."

"What's worse than being killed?"

His jaw clenched and Bethany thought it would be better if she kept her mouth shut before he strangled her. "Nevertheless, you knew of the rules before you ran off on your foolish trip. You should always tell me where you're going—"

"But—"

"I'm guessing you didn't tell me you were taking the horse because you knew I would disapprove." He narrowed his hazel eyes as he walked toward her, bent down on his knees and gave her a long, hard look. "Isn't that right, sweetie?"

"Oh, all right. But I hardly think going on a little trip gives you the right to spank me. Especially since you have already spanked me once. I refuse to allow you to spank me."

He shrugged. "That's fine. Then you can find another place to live. My mother generously offered her home to you for the year, but she is not here right now, and I will not have you breaking the rules left and right. You either take a punishment now, or you can find new lodgings, Miss Fields."

Bethany hesitated. She wasn't getting paid until the end of next week and she currently had less than two dollars to her name. She briefly thought about asking Imogene or Penny for shelter, but Penelope's guest room had been transformed into a nursery and Imogene lived too far away from the schoolhouse.

He tapped his fingers against his forearms. "What is it going to be, Miss Fields?"

Bethany felt a wave of irritation when she noticed he had basically backed her into a corner. "I'll take the spanking. I still think it's silly for you to be upset about such a small thing."

"You can think whatever you want." Peter led her up the stairs to the privacy of her bedroom. "Beth, you were gone for hours. You had me searching like a fool, practically looking under every rock for you."

Bethany smiled. For some reason, the idea of him looking for her, caused her belly to flip in glee. The smile quickly left her lips when he closed the door of her bedroom and she saw the dreaded wooden spoon again. "It's going to hurt," she whined.

"Spankings are supposed to hurt." His voice was without sympathy, but he wasn't cruel, either. He sat on her bed and patted his knee. "Let's get this over with, Beth."

Bethany hesitated; she knew Peter would never truly cause her harm. A spanking wasn't the same as being punched in the face after all, but it wasn't like she was eager to run into his arms to get her bottom tanned. Perhaps being homeless wouldn't be so bad after all.

"Bethany." His dark brows furrowed with a mix of annoyance and impatience. "The sooner you come here, the sooner we can get your punishment over with."

"I still don't know why I'm getting punished in the first place," she grumbled as she grudgingly made her way toward him. He saw her hesitate a bit and in an act of kindness, he draped her over his knee.

A small squeak escaped from her lips as she felt his hard knee on the middle part of her body. She relaxed for a bit when she was finally draped over his knee, but she immediately started squealing when she felt him pulling up her skirt and petticoats and unlacing her very expensive drawers.

"What are you doing?" she squeaked as she tried to push his hands away, but he gently slapped her hands away. "This is hardly proper, Peter! You didn't spank me half naked last time."

"This offense is much worse than last time, sweetheart." He chuckled, apparently ignoring her distress as he placed his large hands on her bare cheeks. She shivered as his thick fingers started stroking her delicate skin. "And if you remember, I told you if you ever misbehaved again, the next spanking would be on the bare."

"A real gentleman wouldn't spank a lady! Let alone, spank her in this position!"

"Well, thankfully, I am not a gentleman. Don't worry, sweetheart, your virtue is safe with me. You'll receive your spanking, and then we can forget about this little scenario. Believe me, you have nothing to be embarrassed about. Your cheeks are lovely."

Bethany turned bright red. She didn't know if he was trying to comfort her or embarrass her. "Oh, just do what you have to do!"

He chuckled. "Music to my ears." She felt him stroking her bottom with the back of the wooden spoon. She didn't know if she should be grateful or dreading it. Surely, his hand was worse than the spoon, right? Bethany just had to grit her teeth and bear it, she would not cry at all—

"Ow!" Her silent promise was quickly broken when she felt the surprisingly hard wooden spoon attack her rear end. The spoon landed five times, so hard and fast that her brain seemed to barely register it.

She started squirming like a fish out of water, but Peter used his free arm to wrap it around her waist, to keep her from getting away. How could such a small spoon hurt so much?

Bethany squealed when the spoon landed again where butt met thigh. She continued trying to get away, knowing her bottom cheeks were probably jiggling as she did. If Peter was bothered by her squirming and protesting, he didn't say anything. Instead, he continue landing the spoon, almost in perfect rhythm, on her defenseless cheeks, no doubt covering them with round, circular spots.

"Young lady, you need get this through your pretty little head," Peter started lecturing as the spoon continued to land with gusto, covering every section of her defenseless derrière and the back of her thighs. "You're no longer in

New York City; you're in Wisconsin and we are not as settled as you're used to. Roaming around by yourself with no chaperone in sight could lead you to getting hurt. I hope you understand that."

"And you need to understand you're a brute!"

Bethany yelped when the spoon started striking the meatier center of her cheeks as she briefly thought that it would have been better if she had bitten her tongue. She silently prayed Peter would end the spanking soon, but it seemed he was just beginning to turn her cheeks crimson.

She could feel the tears threatening to spill at any minute, but she was determined to refuse to let them fall. However, the longer Peter spent peppering her cheeks and no doubt turning them an angry shade of red, the less confident she became of being able to hold her promise.

The tears slowly started to fall, and she no longer cared that she wasn't able to fulfill her promise. Her cheeks were hot and achy, and she didn't doubt they would be sore for days. Peter finally placed the wooden spoon next to the bed as she cried her eyes out. He very gently lifted up her drawers and pulled down her petticoats and skirt. She started crying when the heavy material touched her sore nates.

"Get some sleep," he said firmly as he helped her stand up on wobbling legs, showing no effort to comfort her. "We have church in the morning."

The next morning was Sunday, and ever since Bethany had stepped out of her room to go to church, the blonde had refused to speak to him. Peter knew he should have comforted her the previous night, but he had been too much of a coward to do so.

While he had been spanking her and turning those beautiful, full cheeks a shade of cranberry red, he had felt himself getting hard. The only reason she hadn't realized, was either because she was clueless or because she had been too busy squirming.

If she had been a common whore, Peter would have taken her right then and there, after her spanking. But she wasn't. Bethany was a well-brought up young lady who, no doubt, still had her innocence. If his mother found out he had seduced the schoolteacher they were boarding, she would have killed him. So, Peter had done the next best thing—he had left her in her room crying all night, instead of trying to comfort her, and now he was paying the price.

Bethany had been upset the first time he had spanked her too, but not as mad as she was today. Yesterday's spanking had been harsher than it had been last time, and even though he had used the spoon instead of the belt, he supposed she had a right to act like there was a bee in her bonnet.

She had refused to even look at him during church, instead, spending the whole service squirming on a very hot, punished rear. He had tried poking her once or twice or giving her a cheeky smile, but she had simply glared at him. If they hadn't been in church, she would have probably sworn at him.

It was at this moment, Peter realized he needed to get a woman's advice, because, quite frankly, he didn't understand women and there was no point in making it even worse than it already was.

Thankfully, his sister-in-law, Penelope, was alone. His brother, Derek, was showing off his son, Colin, and Imogene and Stefan hadn't attended church because Stefan was sick in bed with a cold. He left Bethany making dull conversation with Sylvia, a local town resident, while he made a beeline towards Penny.

"I need to talk to you."

Before Penelope could utter a single word in protest, he had gripped her wrist and nearly dragged her to the back of the church. She raised a dark eyebrow, obviously not impressed. "What's the emergency?"

"I need your advice."

"We couldn't do that inside?"

"This is the only time when you don't have a husband or a baby attached to your hip," he admitted with gritted teeth, losing all of his patience.

"Fair point. Now, what can I do for you?"

"I did something, that, uh, might have been the wrong thing to do. Now, I need to fix it before I make it worse."

Penelope took in a deep breath, still looking confused. "Continue."

"I spanked Bethany," he blurted out. There. They couldn't tiptoe about the incident anymore. "She left on horse to Plentville without telling anyone where she was going. You know as well as I how dangerous that could have been."

Penny parted her lips. "Well, it was only one spanking—"

"This is the second time I've spanked her, actually," he said sheepishly. "The first time, she did something indecent."

Penelope placed her hands on her hips as she narrowed her eyes at him. "Are you planning on marrying Bethany? Because even you know better than to put the school-teacher over your knee without plans of commitment."

Peter gaped at her but didn't say anything. He couldn't. She was right; Bethany had a reputation to protect, and he couldn't be spanking her just because she was naughty, sheriff or not. He needed to either leave her alone or drag her to his brother's church to wed.

"Do you love her?" This time, Penelope's voice was gentler, and she was looking at him with pity, which he hated.

"I don't know," he admitted. "It's been years since I felt something for a woman that wasn't just desire. Since the first day we met, Bethany has..." he broke off, looking uncomfortable. He wasn't used to the mushy stuff, especially in front of another woman. "All I know is I don't want her to be involved with another man. Her reputation would be more than safe with me, I promise. This is not something I plan to advertise."

"You don't have to convince me." Penelope looked amused. "Look at you, getting serious about marriage and getting all flustered. I never thought I would see the day."

He wanted to move away from the conversation as soon as possible. The last thing he needed was to get all mushy. "I didn't comfort her last night," he blurted out. "I'm guessing that's why she's mad. I comforted her the first time."

"Perhaps," Penny admitted. "I don't think it's that at all. I surely don't feel like cuddling when Derek spanks me. I'm guessing she's just as confused as you are. You're not courting after all."

"What should I do then? To bring up the topic of courting, she has to look at me first."

"Well, the answer is quite simple. Talk to her."

"Talk to her? That's your advice?"

Penelope shrugged her shoulders, obviously not caring that her answer frustrated Peter. "What do you want me to say? Women are talkative creatures; surely, you don't expect Bethany to respond to brute strength like you do."

"You're not funny."

"Your brother thinks I'm hilarious. Besides, you know I'm right."

Peter stood there for a few minutes before he admitted reluctantly that dear Penny was right. He went to the front of the church and saw that everyone had left. Bethany was waiting impatiently near the wagon. Her arms were crossed as she was glaring at him, reminding him of an angry cat.

"Where were you?" she demanded.

"I needed to take care of something," he replied absentmindedly as he helped her into the wagon. "When we get home, we need to talk."

She stiffened next to him. "I surely don't have anything to say to you."

"Good, because you're going to sit there, and you are going to listen to me."

Bethany gave an exaggerated sigh and pouted for the rest of the trip, every once in a while, squirming on her sore nates. Once Peter had stored away the horse and wagon, he followed her inside his parents' house where Bethany was making tea.

"Can I have a cup?" he asked, even though truth be told, he would have preferred a scotch.

She raised an eyebrow but served him a cup. She brought it to him but not before sitting on the fluffiest pillow she could find. His cock stirred when he thought back to how beautiful her cheeks had looked bouncing over his lap.

"We need to talk." His voice felt dry.

"So, you've said. Twice."

There was an awkward silence which frustrated him to no end. As the town sheriff and the eldest Stevenson brother, people were usually apologizing to him. The blonde was still scowling at him like an angry kitten, and he thought he probably had a minute or two before she started yelling at him.

"I'm sorry," he finally admitted, "about yesterday."

"Are you apologizing because you spanked me?"

"Of course not, Beth. You and I both know you deserved every last swat. After I punished you, I didn't comfort you as I should have. I just left you crying, and I shouldn't have done that. I'm sorry."

For a while, Bethany didn't say anything, then she finally spoke. "Why did you spank me? And why were you so upset I went to Plentville? You may be the sheriff, Peter, but that doesn't mean I should report every small thing to you."

Peter moved his body so he was facing her. "You're a smart girl, Bethany, but sometimes you're too impulsive. Truthfully, you've been impulsive since the first day we met, and don't even try to deny it," he warned when she gave him an unladylike snort. "When I came back and saw you were gone and had taken one of the horses, you struck a fear inside me I didn't even know I had. So many things could have happened, with you running off. A spanking was used to reinforce the warning that that little incident should never happen again. I hate to break it to you, my dear, but you are not a very good listener. Now be truthful with me. Are you mad because I spanked you again, or because I left you crying in your room last night?"

Bethany blushed deep pink as she refused to answer him and instead, placed her eyes firmly on the floor. He moved to the seat next to her in order to be closer to her. Patience, which had never been Peter's strong suit, only lasted about three minutes. He tilted her chin up, using his index finger and thumb. "Answer me, sweetie. Why have you been planning my demise since this morning?"

She was still blushing, but at least she was now

meeting his eyes. "I was mad that you spanked me because I thought you were being overly harsh, but then you just left me there. You didn't do that the first time you, erm—"

"Spanked you?" His lips twitched with amusement at the fact she couldn't say a simple word. "I was in the wrong for that, Bethany, and I apologize. I should have known better. All women deserve comfort after a tanning, even if they did deserve a rosy bottom." He winked at her, causing her entire body to grow red.

"Peter, c-can I confess something to you?"

"Of course."

"I haven't stopped thinking about that night."

"What night, Beth?"

"The night when I ran out of the washing room, and we kissed." Her voice was so low, he wouldn't have been able to hear her if he hadn't been sitting next to her. "I'm sorry. I shouldn't have brought it up."

"No, you should have," he blurted out, suddenly feeling shy himself, which was a rarity for him. He touched her soft lips with his rough fingers. "Did you like how I kissed you, Bethany?"

For a few seconds, she didn't answer, and he petted her cheek. "Answer me, darling. Did you like how I kissed you?"

"Yes," Bethany squeaked. "I've been kissed before, but that time it was different. I liked how you kissed me."

Peter brushed away his annoyance at the thought of other men kissing his Bethany. "Do you want me to kiss you again?"

She gave a sweet little nod.

Peter leaned down and kissed her softly. As soon as his lips touched hers, he felt like a madman, almost as if he had been waiting for her kiss for decades. Bethany returned the kiss with eagerness, which surprised him since she wasn't always the most affectionate.

Their kissing became more intense, and his hands started wandering down the waist of her dress. He knew he should stop, his hands were wandering towards dangerous territory, especially since they weren't exactly engaged. But he couldn't stop. He could only focus on kissing every part of her soft skin. He wanted to kiss, bite, and lick her. Peter wanted to hear her cry out in pleasure as she begged him to stop.

Peter waited for her to tell him to stop. He couldn't blame her if she did. She was a high-born lady, after all, and rolling in the hay with the sheriff of a small town probably wasn't on the top of her list of things she wanted to do.

But Bethany didn't stop him. Instead, Peter watched as she arched her neck, exposing more of her bare neck so that he could kiss it. His fingers removed the ribbon at her neck; he didn't want to run the risk of Bethany throwing a fit, so he barely resisted the urge to rip apart the thick, lace neckline of her dress.

"If you want me to stop, tell me now," he warned her. "Otherwise, I am not making any promises. Are you sure this is what you're happy doing?"

She nodded as her fingers gripped the buttons of his waistcoat. She was almost as eager as he was, and he could be wrong, but he could swear there was twinkle in her eye. "Yes, I am happy doing this. Oh, please, Peter, don't stop."

That was all the encouragement he needed. Within seconds, he had scooped her up in his arms and they were heading to her bedroom at lightning speed. In his excitement, he plopped her on the bed, landing her on her bottom.

She squealed in pain as she glared at him while his hand rubbed her sore flesh.

He gave her a sheepish smile as he crawled on the bed next to her. "I'm sorry. I will be gentler, I promise. I forgot about your bottom."

"I didn't." She sniffed.

"I know. I made sure of that."

She glared at him for a few seconds, but Peter quickly got her thinking of something else as his large hand started to heavily pet her. He touched her soft breasts underneath the thick fabric of her dress. He caressed her sensitive neck with his fingers roughened from years of riding. Every curve of her body that was covered by the dress, was fondled and admired.

Peter was hard. He could feel his manhood threatening to rip out of his pants if he didn't hurry and release it. The crotch of his pants was unbearably tight, but he didn't want to scare her. She was a virgin after all.

He stopped in his tracks. A virgin. Christ. He had never been with a virgin before, in order to avoid being wed against his will. He had always sought the company of loose women or lonely widows when he needed to satisfy himself. Now, he was not dealing with an experienced woman, but an innocent.

Go slow, Peter, he scolded himself as he started helping Bethany remove her clothing. She looked at bit nervous but compliant. After all, he had seen her bare bottom. *The last thing you want to do is make her cry. Make this enjoyable for her.*

Those thoughts quickly went out the window when he saw her naked, and then he only thought about burying himself inside her. He took in her pale, full breasts, her slight belly, and the soft blonde curls between her legs. She looked as beautiful as a Greek goddess. He wanted to say all that and more, but it seemed he could only gape at her like a stunned idiot.

Bethany blushed as her hands immediately went to cover her exposed chest. "No," he blurted out as he gently removed them. "Don't cover them. You're beautiful."

She did as she was told and placed her hands primly on her lap as if she were waiting for tea. Peter wanted to laugh; she looked so prim and proper, even though she was on her bed, naked with an unmarried man and a rosy, red bottom to match.

"Peter," she asked him shyly. "Will it hurt?"

"Yes." He decided to be honest with her. Even though he had never taken a woman's virginity, he knew from drunken talks at the saloon that the first time for a woman was most often always painful. "I'm sorry, darling, there is no way around it, I'm afraid. I'll be as gentle as possible, sweetie. The first time is always the most painful, but after that, Beth, it will feel absolutely wonderful. Do you trust me?"

She nodded as she stared at him. For the first time since he had known her, she was lost for words. Peter started undressing himself, removed his shirt and then his trousers. "You have seen me naked before, darling." He chuckled, enjoying teasing her. "I just hope this time, you don't run away screaming."

Bethany opened her mouth to respond, but nothing came out. Instead, she just stared, her green eyes becoming wider and her face flushing darker pink. She seemed to take in every part of his body, the tanned forearms, the hard chest, and the cock between his legs that had made him famous among his former lovers. After today, he couldn't even think about making love to another woman. After Bethany, it wouldn't feel right.

Her green eyes were still staring at his manhood, and

he didn't have the heart to tease her. "I know it looks daunting, but I will go slow, honey, I promise. I need you to be a brave girl and trust me."

She nodded meekly as he leaned down to kiss her. He wanted to calm her nerves. The kissing helped, and he felt her shoulders relax as she returned the kiss eagerly, her soft breasts rubbing against his muscles.

His hands went towards her breasts as he cupped one of them in his hands, his thumb grazing over the puckered nipple as he felt it go hard underneath his finger. Bethany shivered slightly as her own hands shyly touched his chest, her warm hands soft and small against his rough skin.

Peter felt his erection grow harder with every touch, but he forced himself to be patient. He wanted to be gentle with her, though he wasn't sure how long he would last as his precum was slowly dripping out. His shaft rubbed against her thigh as Bethany rubbed her hot little body against his.

His hand left her breast and traveled to her mound covered in those lovely golden curls. He cupped her womanhood in his large hand, and she let out a surprised squeal as Peter started fondling it.

Her womanhood felt warm and snug, and Peter fought the urge to beg her to be always naked. His thick fingers stroked between her lips before inserting one inside her. Bethany let out a small whimper as Peter kissed her temple. She was unbelievably tight, and he would have to be as gentle as possible in order not to cause her any pain. "Lie on your back," he ordered.

Bethany did as she was told, and Peter went on his knees as he pulled Bethany forward towards the edge of the bed. He pushed her legs apart and leaned forward.

She started screeching, "What on earth do you think you're doing?"

"Pleasuring you," he smirked at her, obviously enjoying the horrified look on her face. "This will make losing your virginity easier on you. Now, lie back down and enjoy, unless you want me to get the wooden spoon again."

Bethany grumbled and did as she was told. Peter wasted no time in pleasuring her as he soon found himself buried between her legs, sucking on the honey nectar that seemed to pool out of her lower lips almost instantly. He used his tongue to caress every inch of her flesh, and her juices seemed never ending the minute he started pleasuring her.

Peter especially loved her plump love lips. He enjoyed biting them and using his tongue to caress every nook and cranny as he swirled his tongue around her engorged clit. He darted his tongue in and out of her rapidly, getting her used to the motions which would soon be happening with his cock inside her.

Bethany let out a small squeak, like a happy kitten, as she gripped the sheets. Peter was careful to stop before she reached her full pleasure. He wanted her to orgasm when she was riding him. After a few minutes of pleasuring her with his tongue, he pulled back.

"This is the part that's going to hurt," he warned her as he helped her to straddle him. Her legs were wrapped around his torso, her rosy bottom sitting on his thighs, and his member was practically rubbing against her lower belly. "But it will only hurt this one time, and afterward, you will feel good, my darling, I swear it. It is a cross all women must bear, unfortunately. Would you like me to go slow as I enter you, or would you prefer me to take your maidenhood quickly?"

"Quickly," she managed to say. "It won't do anyone any good if you prolong the inevitable. I'd rather just get it done and get to the part where I actually enjoy it."

Peter nodded as he kissed her. "There's my brave girl. While I'm taking your maidenhood, you may bite, scream, and insult me as much as you want. I promise you I will not spank you for it."

Bethany nodded as Peter cleared his throat and positioned his rod against her entrance. He instructed Bethany to grip both of his forearms to steady herself and she did as she was told. He entered her slowly as he pierced himself through the untouched flesh. She stiffened slightly when he reached her barrier, but as she requested, he continued going. If he stopped, she was bound to get more nervous.

Peter broke through her delicate barrier in one quick thrust, and she let out a small yelp as she looked at him with wounded eyes. "It's over, sweetie." He pulled out of her and noticed the remnants of her virginal blood on his prick. He silently prayed she would enjoy the remainder of their evening. He didn't want her to spend the entire night in pain. "This next part will be much better, I promise."

She nodded as she lifted her bottom from where it was currently resting on his thighs, and he mused that making love after a spanking was probably not the best combination.

He lowered his finger toward her clit and started rubbing the little pearl. She arched her back while pulling herself forward, nearly throwing her breasts at him. He caught one of them inside his mouth while he continued to rub her clit in slow, circular motions.

Bethany whimpered but did her best not to move as she wiggled her hips to the side. Once he was satisfied that she was wet and ready, he entered her again and started thrusting into her slowly. His mouth was still on her breast, sucking on her sweet nipple while his hands continued to make sure she was getting as wet as she possibly could.

The blonde started panting as she bit back cries of pleasure when Peter led her to her release. He had made love to plenty of women, but making love to Bethany felt different. It felt even more wonderful than it had been in previous times. He enjoyed feeling his cock between those dewy lower lips of hers as he constantly filled her with his manhood. The little cries she made were music to his ears, and she looked at him with almost adoration, even though she obviously hated being told what to do.

He removed his mouth from her breast and then used both of his hands to squeeze those red cheeks, pulling her in even deeper. She was close; he could almost taste it.

"Scream, honey," he ordered as he dug his nails into her back, leaving behind angry, red fingermarks. His thrusts were becoming faster, and he could see Bethany was close to her release. Her cheeks were flushed, and her little mouth was opened as she panted. Peter was close, too, but he didn't want to finish before she did. "I know your body is begging for you to scream."

And she did. It wasn't a loud scream by any means, but it was louder than any scream Peter had heard come from her pretty little mouth. Peter could listen to her screams of pleasure all day as he felt her quivering body in his arms.

"You did good, sweetheart," he managed to say as his heart beat rapidly inside his chest while he patted her back. "You should get some rest. Both of us."

Peter noticed there was blood on the white sheets, the last remnants of her virginity, and made a mental note to take them to the laundry room. Or it might have been easier to just buy new ones.

Bethany surprisingly snuggled next to him. As she buried her face against his burly chest, it was then Peter realized the gravity of the situation. Spanking was one thing, but he had now slept with the prissy schoolteacher who was living with his mother.

"Marry me." The words slipped out of his mouth easily. Words he had never uttered in his life before. Or at least he had never said the words seriously before. It was the least he could do after all. She was a lady, and he hadn't been careful; a baby could be born out of wedlock. He could not allow it.

Funny as it was, he wasn't asking Bethany to marry him simply because it was the right thing to do, but because he truly wanted to marry her. Maybe his brothers and their wives had been right when they said he had feelings for Bethany.

Peter wasn't exactly a sentimental person, but he could safely say he enjoyed her company, he liked teasing her and making her smile, and those lips, those wonderful lips. He could kiss them every hour. Yes, marrying her was what he wanted to do. Besides, he didn't want any other man near her, so the sooner he wed her, the sooner he could let everyone in town know that Bethany belonged to him. His sisters-in-law might say he was acting like a cave man, but he didn't care. He would make an honest woman out of Bethany come hell or high water.

Bethany, who had been starting to fall asleep, threw him a startled look, before she parted her lips and said, "No."

Peter looked at her, perplexed. He had been a flirt for years and wasn't used to being so blatantly rejected. He had to admit, his pride hurt. He stared at her for a while. Bethany squirmed a bit. "Why the hell not? There could be a baby involved," he continued. "It was my mistake, I admit it. I shouldn't have pushed too far, but what's done is done. The proper thing would be to marry."

The blonde threw him a look of pity before she slowly

said, "I can't. Not now. There's something I need to do before I marry anyone."

Peter narrowed his eyes in suspicion, wondering why women insisted on acting so mysterious instead of blurting out what they should say. "What is it? Is this the reason why you went to Plentville?"

She didn't answer him and instead, rested her head firmly against the pillow. "I didn't say I wouldn't marry you," she replied, changing the conversation. "I just said there is something I need to do before I commit to marriage."

Peter stared at her for a while, the sheriff part of him wanting to question her until she confessed, but he knew that would just upset her. Besides, he admitted she had probably gone through more than any woman should on a simple Sunday afternoon.

"All right," he finally said after a while as he stroked her cheek. "Take all the time you need."

Chapter 7

Bethany's poor bottom cheeks were red and swollen from the terrible wooden spoon. She was fully dressed, and Peter would be taking her to school at any minute now, and instead of getting her stuff ready, she was inspecting her red ass in her bedroom mirror.

She let out a hiss of pain as she cradled one sore cheek that peeked through the slit of her drawers. The idea of sitting on her red bottom was enough to make her burst into tears. Damn Peter and his torturous wooden spoon.

Her hands immediately let go of her skirts when she heard an impatient knock on the door. "Let's go, Beth, we're going to be late!"

"Coming!"

She winced as she leaned down to button her shoes. She still felt a little sore between her legs from yesterday, but between receiving a spanking and passionate lovemaking, she wasn't surprised that her entire lower body felt achy.

Bethany slowly made her way downstairs, still processing everything that had happened in only the past two days. She had been spanked, had become a woman at last, and received a marriage proposal. A girl could only handle so much.

Among all the things that had occurred to her in a span of a day, what she could most think about was the marriage proposal. Peter had been upset, but he had been understanding about her rejection and that she wanted to wait. He *had* sprung it on her.

The proposal had been unexpected, so she had said the first thing on her mind, that she had other things to take care off. Which she did. She didn't even want to think about marriage until she found her mother. Though, who knew how long it would take?

She thought about marriage and then about Peter. Would she enjoy being married to Peter? Could she stand the fact that she would more than likely be punished if she was his wife? How did she even feel about him? Yes, he was much older than she was, but when she was with him, it didn't feel like it. He liked teasing her and she had grown to like it, especially when she saw how his lips curled into a familiar grin.

Then she thought about how she had felt when he had been making love to her—protected, cherished, treasured. He had been gentle with her, even though she was a bumbling mess with a sore bottom. Her first time making love had been slightly painful but also incredibly sweet, and Peter had not stopped until she was groaning with pleasure.

Marriage. She had never really thought about it once she came to Wisconsin. Her only thoughts had been on her mother, not on being the sheriff's wife. She shook her head. Marriage proposals should be the last thing on her mind; the only thing she needed to focus on, was her mother.

Now she only hoped she wasn't pregnant. Otherwise, he would drag her to his brother's church himself.

"What took you so long?" he demanded, annoyed.

"A girl needs time to make herself pretty."

"You're already pretty."

Thankfully, he wasn't acting any different than he normally did, for which she was grateful. Most men didn't appreciate being rejected, but he was acting fine with it. A small part of her wondered if he was already regretting proposing to her and she hoped that wasn't the case. Especially since she had been in his arms all night.

Bethany smiled at his compliment.

"How are you feeling?"

"About which part?"

"I'm assuming you're feeling sore all over." He grinned at her. "Do you need me to doctor you up?"

Bethany turned red. "No, thank you."

"So polite. If you're a good girl today, I will place ointment on your rear end after school."

Bethany rolled her eyes as she went outside to get in the wagon and head to the schoolhouse. Both of them remained silent for the rest of the journey to the schoolhouse. Every once in a while, Peter looked back at her in concern, no doubt thinking about last night and the rejected marriage proposal, but truth be told, she had other bigger fish to fry. She needed to find her mother. Once she found out whether she was dead or alive, then she would finally be at peace. She wouldn't have been able to accept Peter's marriage proposal until she had the information she craved, the one that had dragged her from her comfy home in New York to the middle of nowhere Wisconsin.

Bethany looked at her bare left hand. Did this mean she was willing to accept Peter's marriage proposal and become Mrs. Stevenson? She peeked to her left and concluded that being married to Peter wouldn't be so bad. Especially if he made love to her every night like he had last night.

"You're awfully quiet," her soon-to-be fiancé commented. "Is everything all right?"

"I just didn't sleep that well," she lied.

"You were snoring."

"I was not!"

"You were, and my chest was covered in drool."

Bethany scowled at him as he stopped the wagon in front of the schoolhouse. She grabbed her lunch pail and practically jumped out of the wagon like a scared kitten. Peter stared at her in amusement, and she wanted to go into the schoolhouse as if he could see her naughty thoughts that he was at fault for causing.

"Beth?"

"Yes?"

"There's a pillow in the supply closet at the schoolhouse." He winked at her. "We wouldn't want your little buns to get sorer than they already are." Bethany scowled at him, feeling both set of cheeks turn red as she headed toward the schoolhouse. She heard Peter laugh behind her as he reminded her he would pick her up at three.

Once she was inside the schoolhouse, she sighed. She didn't know what to do. All she knew was that teaching was not the only thing on her mind at the moment. The kids were behaving better, but she was a terrible teacher and there was no way around it.

She looked at the ancient clock that had probably been there since the school had been built. The students would be there in half an hour, but the only thing she could think about was her mother, Ruth. Knowing Peter, he wouldn't stop pestering her about marriage, and if there was a baby involved, she knew for a fact that all three of the Stevenson brothers would probably drag her down the aisle.

Bethany needed to find her mother quickly, especially since she knew after the little stunt she'd pulled a few days ago, Peter would have a more watchful eye on her. The brothel, she remembered she hadn't visited it during her last time in Plentville. As much as the idea of going inside a brothel made her sick to her stomach, she had no other choice.

She grabbed a piece of paper from her desk along with a quill and ink and carefully wrote a note to the students, letting them know she was ill and classes would resume tomorrow.

A stagecoach departed to Plentville every Monday at eight o'clock, and if she hurried, she might just make it. She didn't know how she would get home, but she would worry about that later. If no one could give her information about her mother at the brothel, then she would have to make the decision if she should give up the search for her mother or if she wanted to keep searching on her own.

Bethany knew Peter was probably going to kill her once he found out she went out of town unsupervised, but she didn't care. The blonde would gladly take a spanking if she could find any information which would lead her back to her mother.

She rushed out of the schoolhouse and heard the owner of the bakery asking her with concern where she was going in such a hurry, but she didn't answer him.

Peter had just come back from visiting the jailhouse when Deputy Clarkson told him he had a visitor. The visitor ended up being the elderly head of the school board, Mr.

Ingalls, who could hardly walk without his cane, was half deaf, and could barely handle a conversation.

However, the elderly man seemed surprisingly coherent now and he looked angry. "Young man," he said with a shaky voice. "I need to talk to you. The young school-teacher, Miss Fields, is staying with you, is she not?"

"She's staying with my mother and father," Peter corrected him. "Though they are both out of town visiting my uncle at the moment. I've been looking after Miss Fields, making sure she doesn't get into any trouble."

"Well, you've been doing a horrible job, young man." The elderly man wheezed. "Not only have I received complaints from the parents about her terrible teaching skills, but now she is leaving her job without a word to anyone, like a fool."

Peter was immediately alarmed. "What? I drop her off at the school every morning. She was there."

"Well, she left after you did, I'm guessing." Mr. Ingalls blew his nose in his handkerchief. "Mr. Young, who runs the bakery, saw her running to the stagecoach station at a quarter to eight. You might want to have some tighter reins on her, young man. She is dismissed from her position effective immediately. Bad teaching is one thing, but to leave her position without any warning, then that's another. I cannot have an irresponsible young woman teaching our children. I'm assuming you understand."

"Of course." Peter was answering, but his mind was on Bethany. Where was she? Was she hurt? Did the irrespon-sible little chit go running off to Plentville, after he told her specifically how dangerous it was? He gripped his belt buckle. One thing was for certain; he was going to have to tan her little hide. Again.

Mr. Ingalls handed him Bethany's letter of dismissal. "I would have thought a young woman who has received such a grand education would have more sense, but apparently, I was wrong." The elderly man left, mumbling about how terribly irresponsible she was.

Deputy Clarkson, who had just arrived from the post office, looked at his boss with concern. "You okay, Pete? You look pretty angry."

There was something scandalous about visiting a brothel before noon, but Bethany had come all this way and had spent so much money on a ticket, there was no way she could back out now. The sooner she found out information about her mother, the sooner she would be able to return to Redwood.

The brothel, named The Doves, was in poor condition and had obviously seen better days. It looked unkept and dirty, and the idea that her mother had spent most of her life here, made her stomach hurt. Why hadn't her father forced her to go with him? She couldn't help but think that if the same thing had happened to her and Peter, that Peter would have dragged her kicking and screaming.

There was an older-looking man smoking a cigar and he was staring at her fumbling form with a bored expression. "Can I help you?"

"Um, yes, I am looking for the owner of this establishment."

"That would be Madame Alexandra."

"May I speak with her? It shall only take a moment."

The man grunted and told her he would check. She remained there fumbling with her thumbs until he came back and told her she would speak with Bethany. Bethany hurried towards the back office where the man had pointed.

Madame Alexandra's office smelled of cheap perfume, cigars, and whisky. A woman in her fifties, with her face covered in heavy rouge, was at her desk. She looked up at Bethany in surprise. "It's not often I have such a pretty visitor at my door so early in the day. How can I help you?"

"I was wondering… I wanted to inquire about a young woman who worked here about twenty-two years ago. Have you been here that long, Madame Alexandra?"

"Honey, I have run this place for thirty-three years. My sister and I started this place when I was just a young lass of twenty, when we both realized men aren't useful to women unless they are placing money in their pockets. Now, who is this woman you're looking for?"

Bethany hesitated. She wondered if she could trust her, but quite frankly, she didn't have many options left. "The woman I'm looking for is named Ruth. I don't know her last name or if she ever married. My father told me she used to work here."

Madame Alexandra didn't say anything for a few minutes. She leaned forward and turned to stare at her. "She did use to work here. She left ten years ago, though, for Willow Oak. Nice lass."

"Willow Oak?"

"A town an hour away from here. Right smack in between Redwood and Plentville. You would need a horse or stagecoach to get there."

"Thank you. Why did she leave your, erm, fine establishment?"

Madame Alexandra shrugged. "Old age. Women aren't pretty forever, and I'm afraid it was time for her to go. Such a shame too; she was a hard worker. Ruth couldn't get a job here in town, given her reputation, so she left to Willow Oak ten years ago. Don't know if she is still there. Ruthie always wanted to go to Chicago. There it is, my dear, I've given you all the information I have. Now, will you care to explain to me why you're asking for old Ruthie? I don't even know your name."

She took in a deep breath; might as well come out and say it. She refused to be ashamed of her mother. "My name is Bethany Fields. Ruth is my mother. My parents met twenty-two years ago. Ruth gave birth to me, and my father took me to New York. I've only recently found out about her, and I've been looking for her ever since."

Madame Alexandra looked surprised but didn't offer any other comment. Bethany reached into her fancy drawstring purse, pulled out a bit of leftover pin money and handed it to the madame. "Thank you for your help. I shall be going now."

The older woman nodded as she took the money. "Miss Fields, a word of warning. I knew your mother for a very long time. She is not the most affectionate of women. Truth be told, I never thought of her as motherly."

Bethany felt her face flush, though she didn't know if it was from confusion or annoyance. Her voice was cold, reminding her of the old Miss Fields, the one who used to reside in New York and didn't know her mother existed. "Madame Alexandra, though I am grateful for your help, I did not ask for your opinion on the matter."

Without another word, the blonde exited the brothel and headed toward the stagecoach station. She prayed there was a stagecoach to Willow Oak leaving soon. Just the thought of waiting another day to meet her mother, made her stomach hurt.

Bethany was so lost in her own thoughts that she didn't hear the sound of a horse galloping behind her. She felt strong arms around her waist as the person put her on top of the saddle with ease. She raised her hand, ready to slap the kidnapper. "Just what on earth do you think you're doing…" She stopped short when she realized who it was. *Peter.*

If she hadn't been so caught off guard, she would have probably laughed in his face. His hazel eyes were narrowed at her and the veins on his neck and forehead were pulsing angrily. He still had a tight grip around her waist even though she was firmly on the horse.

"What are you doing here?" she managed to squeak out. "How did you find me?"

"Funny, I should be asking you the same thing. Shouldn't you be at work?" he asked sarcastically. "And it wasn't much trouble finding you. I don't know if you've noticed, but the people of Redwood love their gossip. Not to mention you have shown an unusual amount of interest in this town."

"You didn't have to come find me. I would have returned home."

"Actually, honey, I wanted to make sure you were actually alive first and drag you home myself personally." His hands were too close to her bottom for comfort. "I guess I didn't make enough of an impression last time, to drill into your head that running around without supervision is dangerous."

Bethany stiffened. "Oh, believe me, Peter, you've made enough of an impression."

"Well, then I guess I have to make a harder impression this time, don't I?"

Bethany stiffened but didn't offer anything else. She didn't have much of a defense.

"You were fired by the way. Not that you seem to care about showing up for work." He gripped her thigh. "You and I, missy, are going to have a long discussion when we get home. You can count on that."

Fired? Well, she guessed she couldn't be too surprised

by that, especially since she had been doing such a lousy job. The two of them didn't speak for the entire two-hour ride home, though Bethany could practically hear Peter fuming as he wrapped his arms protectively around her as if he were afraid she would jump off the horse and run in the opposite direction.

She wanted to ask him about Willow Oak, but she figured she would wait until he had calmed down. Once they finally reached home, Peter helped her down and gave her a hearty smack on her rump. "Get inside; we'll talk once I put the horses away."

"When you say talk—"

"It means I'm going to be talking while I'm roasting your rump."

Bethany blushed but didn't say anything more as she found her way inside the Stevenson home while Peter headed off to the stables.

Bethany practically walked in circles as she waited for Peter to come back inside. She was in for it now. She was going to get her bottom properly roasted. She knew this was bound to happen, but now that it actually was, she wanted to run in the opposite direction.

She flinched when she saw him come in. His anger had diminished somewhat, but his hand was still too close to his belt buckle for her comfort. "I can explain why I'm constantly running off to Plentville."

"It had better be a good reason if you continue to risk your life and lose your job in the process." He laughed harshly.

She shifted uncomfortably. "It's a long story."

Peter patted his knee, motioning her to join him. "Lucky for you, I have the time."

Chapter 8

"**A**nd that's the entire story," Bethany finished awkwardly as she turned to stare at Peter who was gawking at her with disbelief. "According to Madame Alexandra, my mother should be in Willow Oak, if she hasn't gone anywhere else, I mean. My mother was the only reason for me to come to Wisconsin and take the teaching job in the first place. My father wouldn't help me, so I decided to take matters into my own hands. I'm sorry, Peter, you must believe me when I say I never had any desire to hurt you or cause you worry. I just couldn't sit around and wait for things to fall into my lap."

"You should have told me." Peter frowned in concern. "Beth, I could have helped you from the start, instead of having you run around like a goose with no sense."

"I just wanted to find her by myself," she replied stubbornly. "Besides, my mother worked as a lady of the night, which is not the most respectable job. I didn't want to cause you and your family shame, especially after your mother was so good to take me in."

"Believe me, our reputation is more than safe." Peter

waved her concerns away. "I will take you to Willow Oak in search of your mother as soon as possible. You are not to leave without me, Bethany. Is that understood? I don't want you getting hurt. You've been very lucky when you've gone out on your solo missions, but that stops tonight."

"Fine," she grumbled.

"I don't care if you're annoyed at me. It's for your own good." He hesitated. "You do realize there is a good chance your mother is more than likely gone or deceased, right? She did leave Plentville ten years ago after all."

"I know, but I have to try, Peter. It would kill me if I didn't at least try."

Peter nodded grimly as he stood up. "Now that we've solved that little mystery, let's get to a less pleasant part of our evening. You disobeyed me again, and you had me chase you all the way to Plentville."

"I didn't ask you to come." She snorted.

"Nevertheless, I wanted to make sure you were safe." Bethany gulped as she watched Peter unbuckle his belt. "I told you the last time what would happen if you disobeyed me, did I not? Raise your skirts, drop your drawers, and then bend over the arm of the divan. You're getting ten strokes of my belt."

Bethany's eyes started watering as she clutched her cheeks with both hands. "No, please. I'm still sore from the wooden spoon. I'll be good, I swear."

Peter ignored her last comment. "I know you're still sore from last time, which is why you're only getting ten strokes when you really deserve twenty. Bend over, young lady, unless you want the belt and the spoon."

She let out a whimper as she reluctantly did as she was told, not wanting to get a double dose. It took all her willpower not to burst into tears once she felt the cool air hit her cheeks. She was barely done healing from the last one and here she was, getting spanked again.

Peter gripped the belt in his hand as he stared down at her still pink cheeks. "I want you to count the ten strokes, Bethany," he ordered, and before she could complain, she felt his thick leather belt hit the middle of her plump cheeks rapidly, one after the other.

"One! Two!" she screeched. "Oh, please not so hard, Peter, it hurts!"

"It's supposed to hurt. It's a punishment." Peter raised the belt again, even though Bethany could swear her cheeks were swelling. The belt landed one time across the backs of both thighs, the upper part of her cheeks, and then the undercurve of her bottom where bottom met thigh. It landed hard and fast, leaving behind rectangular prints on her ass from the belt. The thick belt was painful, and Bethany was hardly able to count the stroke before the belt landed again.

"Five more, honey." Peter rubbed his hand against her warm nates, which caused Bethany to burst into tears. "You're being very good during your spanking. I don't like punishing you, but you need to mind me."

The sheriff raised the belt again and landed the sixth stroke harshly against both cheeks. Bethany's cheeks were now deep red and covered with the marks of the belt. The skin was hot and swollen, guaranteeing she would be sleeping on her belly for at least a week.

The seventh and eighth strokes cracked painfully against her lower bottom cheeks. Bethany groaned out the numbers as her bottom wobbled erotically in the air, almost as if waiting for the remaining strokes. Even though she tried avoiding his punishing hand, Peter always managed to whip her where he wanted.

For the remaining two strokes, he pulled her legs apart.

The belt landed unexpectedly on her quim, her love lips and her clit receiving the majority of the stroke. The delicate skin swelled almost instantly, the red strokes from the belt matching her ass. "Nine. Ten." Thankfully, Peter counted the strokes for her. "It's over, baby girl."

Bethany shrieked as she stood up and clutched both cheeks in her hands. She tried to rub the punished skin, but touching it only seemed to make it worse. She hopped around the living room, still crying as she tried to soothe her angry red bottom.

Peter let her cry for a few minutes as she started to embarrassingly dance around the dining room with her skirts pulled up while her angry red cheeks jiggled in the air and she tried to rub away the soreness with little success.

Her eyes were dripping with her tears, and she silently vowed to be good enough to never earn the belt again. She couldn't even be mad at Peter this time, because she had disobeyed him again.

Peter tossed the belt across the room and opened his arms. "Come here, baby."

Bethany scurried toward him and buried her face in his chest as she continued crying. Peter whispered sweet nothings in her ear as he stroked her back. Once she had finally calmed down, Peter started to place both hands under both globes and push them up.

Bethany, sensing where he was going with this, started squirming. The idea of lying on her back after being whipped was enough to get her to burst into tears. "Oh, please, no, Peter, I'm too sore."

"Don't you desire me, like I desire you, baby?" he asked as he started nibbling on her ear. She could feel the bulge of his erection pressing against her mound.

"Of course, I do." Even though she was the only one

who was half naked, she could feel her own sweet nectar dripping down her thighs. "But I don't want to lie on my back."

Peter chuckled. "There are other ways to make love, sweetie. We don't even have to be fully dressed. Come here." He led her, half naked, to the bare wall and pressed his back against it. He pulled his clothes down from his lower body and motioned her to come forward.

She did as she was told, her womanhood tingling at the thought that she was soon going to be making love to Peter. How did women not get addicted to making love every night? "Press both of your hands on my shoulders," he instructed her. "Now raise your leg." Bethany did, and he gripped his hand underneath her thigh, lifting her, then he did the same to the other one.

Peter nearly ripped apart her dress as he pierced her with his already hardened cock. Bethany let out a surprised groan when she felt his manhood enter her, stretching her apart as she accommodated him. She squeezed her thighs together as she started moving her hips in circular motions, riding him.

The sheriff squeezed the backs of her thighs. "I love how your tight little quim milks my cock every time I'm inside you." He whispered in her ear, "Do you like it when I'm buried inside you, Bethany?"

Bethany blushed but nodded.

"Say it, Beth."

"I like it when you're inside me." Bethany moaned as he raised her thighs and pulled her forward so that her pleasure pearl rubbed against his lower belly. She felt the dark curls from his pubic area tickle her womanhood.

Bethany felt her wetness increase, the more he rubbed the hard muscles of his stomach against her love button. She wouldn't be surprised if her quim was a slippery mess, especially since she was sure she was currently coating both of their thighs with her wetness.

"Please marry me," Peter whispered in her ear with his cock still buried inside her. The tears had dried on her cheeks, but her eyes were slightly swollen. He squeezed her sore butt cheeks as he buried himself even deeper inside her, causing her to cry out. "I know I promised you I'd be patient, but you running around like a madwoman has made me quite impatient. Marry me, Beth, please. I love you."

Bethany choked on a laugh as she turned to look at him. She then nuzzled her face against his scratchy beard. "How can you tell me you love me after you've turned my ass bright red?"

"I love turning your little butt pink too, especially when you deserve it." He kissed the tip of her nose as he started stroking her engorged clit. "So, what do you say, Beth? Will you become my little housewife?"

Bethany nodded as she continued rubbing her mound against his lower belly, following the rhythm of his manipulative fingers. "Yes, I will marry you." She turned to look at his hazel eyes that seemed to be smiling at her. "And, Peter, I love you too."

Chapter 9

The next seven days felt endless to Bethany as she waited for her fiancé to take her to Willow Oak. Her fiancé. It felt funny to even think about it, let alone say it out loud, considering she couldn't stand the sheriff when she had first arrived in Redwood. As her green eyes stared at the engagement ring Peter had given her, a gold band with a diamond in the center and smaller stones surrounding it, she couldn't help but feel sad.

She wanted her mother at her wedding. A mother should be present at her daughter's wedding, should she not? She wanted to invite her father as well. Even if the man was still cross at her, she just knew her dear papa would want to be at her wedding. He had been wrapped around Bethany's finger since day one.

Peter wanted to get married as soon as his parents returned to town, and he had already sent them a letter. She had told him she wanted her mother there, but Peter had pointed out that they first had to find her. Peter had been too busy during the week to take her to Willow Oak and during the weekends, he was helping Stefan get the cattle and the ranch ready for winter.

Even though it had only been a week, she had been growing desperate. Since she had been fired from her job, Bethany had been playing the role of housewife, which would be her official role when she and Peter married. Peter told her to think of this as her trial period. She wasn't bad at cleaning, but she hadn't done much cooking or her own laundry before.

In order to distract her from looking for her mother and to teach her homemaking skills, Peter had dropped off Imogene and baby Daisy every morning.

"I'm so glad we finally get to be real sisters," Imogene squealed as Bethany played with baby Daisy on her lap. "I'm so happy you and Peter are getting married. If I'm being honest, we were quite worried about him. We thought he would remain a bachelor forever." When Bethany didn't answer, she poked her on her side. "Beth, are you all right?"

"Yes," Bethany admitted as she tickled Daisy on her belly. The baby squealed in glee. "I'm sorry, Imogene, I'm being rude. I'm just feeling a bit distracted lately."

"You're thinking about your mother, aren't you?" Imogene blushed. "I'm sorry for blurting it out. Peter mentioned it. I shouldn't have pried."

"No, it's all right. Peter promised he would take me to Willow Oak, but he's been so busy. It's just this urge I feel. I know I may sound ridiculous, but I need to make sure she's all right. I just need to see her at least once. All this waiting around seems endless, and it's hard to be patient."

Imogene didn't say anything for a few minutes, then she spoke. "There is a stagecoach that leaves for Willow Oak today at eleven, in exactly forty minutes. That should give you a few hours to look through Willow Oak for your mother. Penny used to live in Willow Oak, and she mentioned there is a daily stagecoach that leaves at three for people who catch the train from Redwood. Peter doesn't have to know you were gone at all. Go."

Bethany stared at her. "Really?"

"Yes, really. Go find your mother. I lost my mother when I was born, and I would give anything to see her again." Imogene took her daughter from her lap. "Now go, before I chicken out and change my mind. Your bottom is not the only one that's going to end up sore if this goes horribly wrong."

Bethany grinned as she kissed Imogene and Daisy on the cheek and rushed out the door. Stagecoach tickets were expensive, but she still had some of her pin money left from her father and the little money she'd earned during the short time she had worked as a schoolteacher.

If it meant she could see her mother again, Bethany would eat cold gravy and biscuits for a month straight.

Please, Lord, Bethany silently prayed as she practically ran down the hill towards town, *let me find my mother.*

It turned out Willow Oak was slightly bigger than Plentville and the terrain Bethany had to cover, therefore, was much larger. After she arrived in town, the first place she went to ask for her mother's whereabouts was the mercantile and the post office, the places people from both genders usually frequented.

However, no one seemed to have heard of a middle-aged woman named Ruth who had arrived from Plentville ten years ago. The lady who ran the post office told Bethany they've had so many people come and go throughout the years, they hardly kept track anymore.

Her belly started grumbling at almost two o'clock in the afternoon, and feeling defeated, Bethany planned to get a bite to eat at the local café before heading back to Redwood. She didn't want Imogene to get spanked because of her, especially since she knew Stefan could be quite stern.

Bethany slumped on a chair at an empty table as a scrawny, pinch-faced woman with ashy blonde hair that was slowly turning gray approached her to take her order. "Can I help you?"

"I would like a cup of tea and a bowl of soup please." Bethany looked at the grouchy woman. The woman looked older, and she was bound to see many people come and go at the café. "Have you always lived in Willow Oak, ma'am?"

"Ten years or so," the woman responded absentmindedly. "Would you like a slice of bread for your soup?"

"Yes, please." Bethany practically pounced on the woman. "By any chance, do you know a woman named Ruth? She was, erm, friends with Edwin Fields back in Plentville?"

The woman's brow furrowed in surprise. "Edwin Fields, why I haven't heard that name in years. How do you know him? You were probably still in your nappies when we met." She placed the pot of tea down. "I'm Ruth, well, my middle name is anyway. My first name is Margaret."

Something inside Bethany clicked as she looked at the woman, this time a bit more closely. She took in the woman's blonde hair that, even though was slowly turning gray, was the same shade as her own. They shared the same green eyes and the pert nose Bethany was so proud of. The woman in front of her had once been a great beauty but now looked haggard, old, and defeated.

Before she could stop herself, Bethany wrapped her arms around the woman. "Thank God, I finally found you. I'm Bethany."

"Why are you hugging me?" Ruth pushed her away, looking both annoyed and confused. "Is that name supposed to mean anything to me?"

Bethany pulled back, looking embarrassed. Probably, hugging a complete stranger wasn't the best plan, especially when she hadn't even explained what she was doing here.

"I'm Bethany Fields," she explained again. "The daughter of Edwin Fields and you. I'm your daughter, Mother. Oh, it feels so good to say that. I came all the way from New York to find you. I'm so sorry I haven't searched for you until now, but father didn't—"

"Not here," Ruth said in a low tone as she gripped Bethany's arm and practically pulled her outside the empty café. Once she had cornered Bethany into an alleyway, she glared at her. Bethany's lower lip trembled as she stared at the angry woman. This hadn't been the reunion she had been expecting. Ruth stared at her for a few minutes before declaring, "You really are my daughter. You look just like me when I was a young woman. It seems like such a long time ago."

"Twenty-one years exactly." Bethany started feeling excited again. Of course, her mother was just feeling a tad overwhelmed. "Oh, I'm so glad I found you. It has been quite difficult, but I—"

Ruth interrupted her, her voice flat when she did. "You shouldn't have come. I didn't want to meet you. Why else do you think I gave you to Edwin over twenty years ago?"

Bethany's throat felt tight as she tried to come up with an explanation. "I know you used to work in a brothel, and you probably gave me away to protect me, but I'm here now. I'm older and you don't have to protect me anymore."

"How much did your father tell you about me and our history?"

"Not much."

"I figured. Edwin always knew how to avoid uncomfortable conversations." Ruth's voice became soft, and she was looking at Bethany with pity. "Edwin and I met when he was a young man and I was working in a brothel in Plentville. I unexpectedly became pregnant with you. I wanted to get rid of the baby. Madame Alexandra promised me there was a woman who could do it, but Edwin begged me not to. I was a young fool, and I listened. After I gave birth, your father begged me to marry him, and I refused. I did not want to spend my entire life in a stuffy New York city ballroom, and I liked being my own person, obtaining my own money with no strings. What I'm trying to say is I never wanted a baby. I've never wanted motherhood. I don't want you, Bethany. I don't want to get to know you. I don't want to be your mother. I'm sorry you came all this way for nothing, but I want nothing to do with you."

Miss Field's eyes watered as she looked at the woman she had been searching for and who had dismissed her in less than five minutes. "But you don't even know me. You could get to know me and I'm sure you'll like me."

"Not likely. You're wasting your time, so please don't make this any harder than it has to be. You're a grown woman and, by that ring on your finger, engaged. You should be someone's mother, not trying to search for the one who didn't even want you."

Before she could even stop herself, Bethany felt the tears pouring down her face. Her entire body shook with her sobs. She had come all this way, left her father, left her home, taken a job she didn't even want, all for her mother, and it turned out she didn't even want her.

Ruth looked uncomfortable. "Listen, I have to go, or I could lose my job. Go back to New York, Bethany. Edwin is a good man; he can love you in a way I never can."

Bethany didn't respond; she just continued crying as Ruth left. She felt raindrops hit her cheeks, but she didn't brush them off. It felt like the sky was crying along with her.

Chapter 10

"You didn't have to come all this way," Peter admitted to his younger brother as both men made their way to their parents' home. "I would have gladly taken Imogene and Daisy home."

"I don't mind. Besides, I want to see my girls." Stefan patted his older brother's shoulder. "And it gives me time to congratulate you on biting the bullet and marrying."

Peter snorted. "You don't have to sound so surprised. I did say a few months ago that I wished to marry, did I not?"

"You did," Stefan mused. "Though I must admit, I didn't expect you to get married so soon, and to Bethany of all people. Don't misinterpret me, she's very sweet and lovely, but you did mention you wanted someone more demure and serious."

Peter shrugged. "The spoiled chit wormed her way into my heart. I just hope this thing with her mother gets resolved soon. You and I both know it's probably not a good thing if the woman has not tried to contact her in twenty-one years."

"Perhaps Bethany's father forbade it."

"Perhaps."

The two men entered their parents' house, and when they did, Imogene, who had been soothing a crying baby Daisy, nearly jumped in the air. There was a strange, wobbly smile on her face and Peter could easily tell she was guilty of something. Imogene was a terrible liar and knew better than to lie to either Stevenson brother. Peter knew she would never place her daughter in any danger, so unfortunately, that only left one final answer. Bethany.

Peter looked around the room, calmly trying to control his temper. "Where is she?"

"Who?" Imogene asked, feigning innocence.

"You know very well who." Stefan raised a dark eyebrow as he stared at his wife in warning. "Where is Bethany, sweetie? Is she upstairs taking a nap?"

Imogene shook her head, immediately caving under the pressure of her husband's warning glance. If there was something Stefan didn't tolerate, it was lying, something she knew very well. "No, she's at Willow Oak. She took the stagecoach there. I just saw her so worried about her mother, I didn't think it would be bad if she went to take a quick peek in Willow Oak to see if she found something. She promised to come back soon, but she's still not back and I'm getting worried."

Peter let out a series of curses, not caring that it was an example of bad manners in front of his sister-in-law and niece. *Dammit, Bethany*. Couldn't she think first before she started running in every direction for a woman she had never even met?

Stefan shook his head as he turned to look at his wife. "That was very naughty, Imogene. You know better, especially after what you've gone through. Looks can be deceiving. There was a reason Peter wanted Bethany to stay put. Both of you should have listened."

Imogene looked at Peter apologetically. "Peter, I am so sorry. I didn't think—"

Peter didn't finish hearing Imogene's apology. Instead, he left the house in a hurry and grabbed his horse. Willow Oak was an hour away, and it was already dark. Dammit. Surely, if Bethany had taken the last stagecoach, she would have been here by now, right?

He rode to Willow Oak as fast as he could. He would've ridden faster if he wasn't worried he was going to end up injuring his horse in this dreaded cold. Peter lifted his heavy coat to shield his face from the rain drops which were quickly dropping from the sky.

The idea of Bethany being in this cold and rain, nearly caused him to go mad. It was too damn cold for any decent person to be out, let alone his Bethany. Many thoughts started entering his mind, most of them negative. What if she was hurt? What if her mother had turned out to be a horrible person? What if someone tried to attack her when they saw she was unchaperoned?

He relaxed only slightly when he saw the town of Willow Oak quickly approaching. There were several trees at the entrance of the town, and Peter saw a small bundle curled up against the large tree trunk. At first, Peter thought it was an old potato sack, but then he saw it had arms and legs. Blonde hair.

"Bethany!" he nearly roared.

But the bundle didn't move, even though he was sure it was her. What was the little fool doing sleeping in the rain? He got off his horse and went towards her, and she still did not stir.

Bethany was in a deep sleep. Peter frowned as he took a

closer look at her. Was it his imagination, or did she look flushed from fever? She had been complaining about a sore throat just the day prior.

"Beth." He tried to gently shake her. "Beth, wake up please."

But she did not move, though she did stir a bit, which was better than nothing. Right now, he just had to get her home and into some dry clothes, then he would call Dr. Moore.

Peter picked her up in his arms, hoping she would wake up, but she didn't. She simply stirred as the rain continued pouring down. Peter felt his throat tightening. She would be all right, he tried to tell himself, she had to be.

By the time Peter had undressed Bethany out of her wet clothes and into a nightgown, she was burning up with a terrible fever. The kind of fever that caused her entire body to shake from chills and for the pale skin to turn an angry, hot red. Peter had left her safely tucked into her bed as he nearly ran all the way into town to get the doctor.

Dr. Moore came almost immediately, and Peter had a feeling that it was brute strength and a demanding attitude that had inspired the good doctor to come to the Stevenson home without any questions. The last thing anyone wanted to do was anger the town sheriff.

Even though Dr. Moore asked him to wait outside to give the unconscious young lady some privacy, he had refused and told him curtly that he was the young lady's fiancé, and he would stay as he saw fit. The doctor raised a dark eyebrow but didn't comment any further as he inspected the patient.

He listened to her chest, had Peter flip her on her belly to take her temperature rectally, and then forced awful smelling willow bark tea down her throat, which caused Bethany to choke out in disgust from the taste.

After making sure she was safely tucked into her bed, Peter reluctantly followed Dr. Moore outside. "How is she?"

"She has quite a fever, and riding around in the rain for an hour didn't help her case. She's lucky she didn't develop pneumonia," the doctor blurted out. "The tea should help with the fever and to avoid congestion in the lungs. I'll come check on her tomorrow. If the tea doesn't work, I have a tonic that can help. You need to keep her in bed, Sheriff Stevenson, and make sure she's bundled up and drinking plenty of liquids when she's awake. That will help her prevent pneumonia, or worse. Make sure you take her temperature every four hours; if it's too high, contact me immediately. We might have to give her a cold bath to help reduce the fever. Let us hope it doesn't come to that. I'll come check on her in the morning. Get some rest if you can."

"I don't think it will be possible," he responded dryly. "Thanks for coming, Doctor. I apologize if I was a bit harsh."

"All is forgiven. We have all acted irrational when we were worried about someone."

"I don't have a thermometer."

"I have an extra one in my bag along with a jar of salve."

For the next two days, Peter played nursemaid, hardly leaving Bethany's bedside, and leaving Deputy Clarkson in charge. He hardly slept, preferring to look at her closely, especially at night, in case her fever rose. This often happened as he watched helplessly while her entire body seemed to become as hot as a furnace. Sweat would bead down her forehead, and she would shift uncomfortably in bed as she tried to find a cool place on the sheets. She was in pain, and Peter felt helpless and foolish because there was nothing he could do to stop it.

When he wasn't bathing her forehead with a cool washcloth, he was trying to force feed her some broth and tea. Though the reality was Peter could count on one hand how many times she had woken up, and when she did, she barely said anything coherent before she returned to a deep slumber.

His sisters-in-law had offered to help, but he had refused, too paranoid she would succumb to her illness to let anyone else handle it. Besides, Penelope and Imogene each had a small baby, and he would feel terrible if either his niece or nephew fell ill.

On the third day of his vigil, Peter could barely keep his eyes open as he continued to stare at Bethany. Her fever had finally broken a few hours ago. Although Dr. Moore had said she was out of the woods, he would not be satisfied until he saw her lips open again and he heard her sweet voice.

He had just been nodding off when he heard her stir. Her green eyes opened dazedly as she blinked at him in confusion. Her voice sounded hoarse and dry as she said his name, "Peter?"

Bethany reminded him of a broken, tired doll. Her face was pale, there were dark circles under her eyes, and her usually pink lips were nearly white. It reminded Peter how close he had come to losing her, and if she hadn't been so weak, he would have spun her in his arms.

Peter choked on his response, unsure of the words to say as he immediately pulled her into a hug, nearly crushing her. Bethany fidgeted a bit before she allowed him to embrace her. "Thank God." He ran a hand through her blonde hair. "How I've longed to see you awake."

Chapter 11

"Are you hungry?" Peter sat at the edge of Bethany's bed watching her intently as she sipped her tea. He studied her pale face, the sunken cheeks, and the dark circles under her eyes. He wished he could have the doctor around every minute of every day, to make sure she was all right or, at the very least, his mother. She would know what to do. "Penelope and Imogene brought all sorts of things. Surely, you want something other than toast—"

"Toast is fine for now," Bethany assured him as she finished her tea and took a bite of her toast. The next few minutes were full of uncomfortable silence. Peter wanted to ask her a million questions, but he also did not want to overwhelm her.

Finally, he couldn't hold off any longer. "I found you leaning against a tree in the outskirts of Willow Oak," he blurted out. "It was raining, and you were passed out from fever and sickness. What happened, Beth?"

Bethany shrugged and replied flatly, "I disobeyed you and took a stagecoach to Willow Oak to find my mother."

Her green eyes suddenly widened with worry. "Oh, no, is Imogene—"

"Imogene is fine. She knows what she encouraged you to do was naughty and Stefan made sure she paid the price for it."

"She shouldn't be spanked because I broke the rules."

"Missy, you have your own hide to worry about." He patted her hand. "Don't get agitated, Beth. The doctor says you need to rest for the next few days at least. Now tell me calmly what happened."

For a while, Bethany did not speak, and when she did, her voice was so hollow and broken, Peter immediately wanted to lift her into his arms and make her feel better. "My mother didn't want me." Her green eyes welled up with tears as she turned to look at him. She was looking so sad and miserable, like a kitten caught in the rain, and Peter wanted to slap her mother for making her so sad.

For the next twenty minutes, Bethany told Peter everything that had happened between her and her mother. With each word, she looked more sad and tired, though Peter suspected it was also from her illness.

"By the time I finally realized I'd been rejected, the last stagecoach had left. I didn't have enough money for an inn, and I didn't want to worry you and Imogene. I was planning on walking back to Redwood when I decided to wait under a tree for the rain to stop. I must have passed out. I don't know why I'm so sad." Bethany finished her tea. "I didn't know the woman, and now I know why my father tried to shield me away from her, out of kindness, rather than cruelty."

"She is still your mother. You had such high hopes, and it's all right to feel disappointment after she turned out to be someone you weren't expecting." Peter squeezed her hand. "I don't know what else to say, darling. I have never been good with emotions. Is there anything else I could say that would make you feel better?"

Bethany shook her head. "Your presence is more than enough. Peter, I'm sorry I went behind your back. Again. I know I deserve a whipping and I won't put up a protest this time."

He chuckled softly as he kissed her clammy forehead. "You were very naughty," he agreed. "But you went through a terrible ordeal and right now, I just want you to focus on getting better, not dreading being over my knee. So, for this incident, I will not spank you, but don't get used to it, Beth. As your future husband, I feel the need to warn you that I am not usually so tenderhearted."

Bethany laughed before she slumped against his chest. "I'm so tired, Peter."

"I know, baby." He pushed her back onto the soft pillows, and she fell asleep almost immediately. "I'll be right here if you need anything."

———

The next few days were surprising for Bethany Fields. First of all, she had no idea the intimidating Peter Stevenson could be an excellent nurse. Second, he was starting to annoy her terribly.

At first, she had practically swooned at the way he brought her meals in bed and tucked her in with a good-night kiss every night. Even though he insisted on taking her temperature every four hours in the most embarrassing position, with her bottom in the air and a thermometer buried deep inside her, he still did it in the most loving matter.

However, by day five, Bethany was convinced her fiancé was slowly driving her insane. Even though she was as right as rain now, despite her pale disposition and sunken cheeks, he still treated her as if she were as frail as a newborn kitten, hardly letting her out of bed except to use the necessities. Bethany was quite frankly sick of it and wanted to at least be allowed downstairs for a change of scenery.

The other problem that arose at still being treated as if she were an ill woman was that Peter had refused to make love to her, even though she'd begged, whined, and fluttered her eyelashes. That was the worst part of his constant fussing.

"I am truly feeling better," she attempted to convince him as she tried to be content with the heavy petting of his hand over her nightgown-covered thigh. "Please, Peter. I miss you."

"I'm right here," he lightly teased her, though he didn't push her back into the pillows and ravish her like she so desperately wanted him to do. "We should wait."

"What on earth for?" she demanded, not caring that she sounded brash and as desperate as a wanton. "We're engaged to be married, and it's not like we've not done it before."

"You're still sick," he scolded her gently as he started nibbling on her bottom lip.

"I *was* sick. I'm better now."

He paused for a moment as he patted her knee. "Get dressed. I'll take you riding with me. You could use some fresh air to pinken your cheeks."

Bethany practically ran to get dressed at the mention of getting out of bed. Within minutes, she was dressed, firmly placed on a saddle, and Peter had his arms around her like a cocoon as he held the reins tightly. Peter was making the horse gallop slowly, but she didn't mind. It was just nice not to be cooped up.

She rested her head against his muscled chest and closed her eyes, feeling the light sun on her face. Fall would soon be over, and then the dreaded winter would come. Bethany hated winter and the cold in general.

"How are you doing, Beth? About your mother, I mean?"

"I am still feeling a bit sad. No one likes to be rejected, even by someone they barely met." She sighed. "But she is still my mother, I think that's what hurts the most, that my own mother rejected me. I was a fool for not listening to my father."

He kissed the back of her head. "You're not a fool for having hope. And while you were reckless in your pursuit of her, you were also brave."

"Do you really think so? I just wish I didn't feel so silly. I did so many things to find that woman, and she didn't even want me."

"I could take your mind off things."

"How so?"

"I could tell you about the deliciously sinful things I am going to do to you once we are properly married."

A smile appeared on her lips as she raised her head up to look at him. "What sort of things?"

He flashed her a smile as he started whispering in her ear in that husky voice of his, "Oh, there are many things I will do to you. Especially this sweet little bottom." He cupped her round cheeks in his hands as he started squeezing the round globes. "I would squeeze it and bite it and spread it so I can bury myself in your cheeks."

"Peter!" she squealed, quite regretting the direction this conversation was going, but also secretly curious. "That is positively sinful."

"It's not sinful if it's to your wife." He pinched her earlobe teasingly. "Besides, if you remember correctly, my darling fiancée, you were behaving like quite a peeping Tom when we first met."

"I was not! I just wanted to get some sleep!"

Peter rolled his eyes playfully as he pulled down her dress slightly, to expose her bare shoulders to the chilly night air. "Sure, you did! Maybe you just wanted to experience for yourself what I was doing to someone else. You know what else I want to do? I want to place my cock between these beautiful breasts of yours and rub them against it up and down, until my seed spreads all over your chest. Your face is so red, Beth. Maybe you are too pure for my sinful little heart."

Bethany didn't want to admit that this turned her on. It was just too improper. Too naughty. Just too intriguing. She wanted to try all those things Peter wanted to do with her. Just imagining them, caused her legs to shake and her womanhood to throb on top of the saddle. If Peter ever tried any of those things on her, she was sure she would faint.

"Would you like to hear more, Beth?" he murmured in her ear.

She nodded.

"Say it for me, doll."

"T-tell me what else you will do to me."

"There's my good girl. Well, I would, of course, bury myself inside you, and with every thrust, I would run my tongue on those perfect pink nipples of yours. Or maybe I would just spend hours holding your little body against my chest as I spread your legs and rubbed the love button between your legs until you reached your pleasure, and I would do it over and over again until you would feel so tired, you would have no choice but to sleep in my arms. How does that sound, sugar?"

She didn't say much for a few seconds; she didn't know

what to say. But then she parted her lips before she let out a small squeak. "I would love that very much."

He let out a loud laugh which reminded her of loud church bells. She loved to hear him laugh and hoped she would hear it for a very long time to come. "Don't fret, Miss Fields. We will soon be married, and I will hardly let you leave my bed. Now let's get you back to bed before you catch your death."

The prospect excited her as they rode back in comfortable silence while Bethany tried to ignore the wetness dripping down her thighs. She gave a silent prayer of thanks that she was going to be married to this man, even if she did get her bottom roasted from time to time.

As they approached the house, Bethany frowned as she saw two people standing in front of the house carrying suitcases. They hadn't been expecting any visitors.

"Peter, I think there's someone at the house."

The smile left Peter's face as he looked at the two people walking towards the house. He went forward, silently telling Bethany to stay put. "It's my parents. They're home."

They approached Mr. and Mrs. Stevenson who both smiled at them. It felt good to have them home. Mrs. Stevenson kissed each of them on the cheek. "Oh, it's so good to see both of you. How have both of you been since we left?"

Peter cleared his throat as he held up Bethany's hand to show off her engagement ring as she shyly tried to bury her face in Peter's shoulder. "Well, Mother, quite a lot has happened."

Chapter 12

"**A**re you sure it's not bad luck, not getting married in white?" Bethany looked at the pink material sprawled on the floor. Penelope and Imogene were helping her create her wedding dress while the babies slept. The three women were spending the evening at the elder Mr. and Mrs. Stevenson's home. "Most women nowadays get married in white."

"Not everyone. White dresses and dust don't always go together." Penelope struggled with the needle and thread. "You will look lovely in pink. Besides, there is no more white dress material left and Peter is anxious for you to be married. He was just waiting for Bonnie and Isaiah to come back."

"I know." Bethany gave a little sigh. She didn't really care about the color of her dress. She would get married in her nightgown if it meant she could marry Peter. She had other things on her mind.

Currently, Mr. and Mrs. Stevenson were at Peter's own house in town, making sure the repairs on the roof were properly done and that everything was ready for Bethany's arrival in a week after they had been properly wed.

Mr. and Mrs. Stevenson had been surprised when Peter and Bethany had announced their engagement, but then relief had settled in when they realized their oldest son was finally getting married. Mrs. Stevenson had been fussing over Bethany, making sure the young woman had everything needed for her wedding and for her new home before the week was up.

Bethany happily realized that while her own mother was not part of her life, her mother-in-law was happily fussing over her and welcoming her to the family. She realized she could have quite a happy life with her husband and her in-laws.

"Are you sure the dress will be done by Saturday?" she asked Imogene worriedly.

Imogene nodded as she started stitching the delicate lace around the collar of the dress. "You have my word. I am an expert when it comes to sewing."

"It's true," Penny told her. "When Colin was born, I was presented with no less than ten blankets."

Imogene shrugged modestly. "I was on bed rest during the last month of my pregnancy. I needed to do something."

Penelope smiled as she fussed with the starched collar of the dress. She had never been very good at sewing, but she was excellent at managing a household, and she was an excellent cook who was very patient with Bethany, who managed to burn water.

"How lucky we are," Penny managed to say. "To be able to laugh and joke, all of us together. How odious it would be if we did not get along."

Imogene giggled as she looked through her box filled

with buttons, to find a pretty one for Bethany's dress. "Or if we were all shrews. The three terrible Stevenson wives."

"I'm sure our husbands sometimes agree we're pretty terrible,"

Imogene rolled her eyes. "They are not saints themselves. I am still surprised Stefan insisted on taking Peter to the saloon to celebrate. It is so unlike him." Her husband was the most serious of the brothers, and Bethany had only seen him smile when he was in the company of his family.

"I'm sure they just wanted a quiet place to share a drink. Redwood is so small, I assume it can be quite difficult for men to find enjoyment." Bethany bit her lip as she looked at Imogene apologetically. "Are you sure there will be no indecent activity going on?"

Penelope snorted. "Believe me, nothing indecent will be going on with my husband, the pastor, tagging along. My husband is almost too levelheaded for his own good. The most that is going to happen is they drink one too many glasses of whisky."

Imogene let go of her sewing to put on the kettle for a cup of tea. "Let's take a break from sewing. I'm exhausted."

Penelope and Bethany joined her at the table for a cup of tea and cookies. Once they were settled in, Imogene wiggled her light eyebrows at her. "Are you excited over your wedding night?"

"Imogene," Penelope scolded.

"What? I'm just curious. Maybe she wants some advice for her first time."

"I don't need advice." Bethany felt her cheeks turn a shade of dark crimson red. "It turns out, Peter is quite the expert teacher."

Imogene let out an excited squeal before she looked at Penelope, who was quietly munching on a cookie. "You don't seem surprised by this."

"It's because I'm not." Penelope gave an apologetic shrug. "I figured since he smacked her bottom more than once, they had already done the deed. No offense, Beth, but I doubt even Peter could have resisted such a temptation."

Bethany didn't consider herself a bashful person, but even she was feeling slightly shy at the brunette's blunt frankness. She simply drank her tea to avoid saying anything.

In an effort to make her feel better, Imogene pulled her into a hug, "Oh, don't be embarrassed, Beth. We have all gotten our butts smacked once or twice."

Bethany lowered her head, ashamed, suddenly remembering Imogene had gotten whipped on her own butt because of her. "Oh, Imogene, I am sorry. I never did quite apologize for putting you in such a difficult predicament with Peter and Stefan."

She had been meaning to apologize much sooner, but then she had gotten sick, and it had been a while since Peter had let her out of his sight. Then Mr. and Mrs. Stevenson had come back, and Peter had become insistent that they married sooner, rather than later, and she had become engulfed in wedding preparations. Thankfully, the blonde didn't hold on to resentment.

The first Mrs. Stevenson shook her head. "Oh, don't you even worry about it, Beth. I've gotten my behind spanked a few times. It was worth it if it allowed you some closure," she finished awkwardly.

The room was silent as Bethany thought back to her mother. She had thought that after a few days, her mother's rejection would have hurt a bit less. In reality, it still hurt quite badly. Once or twice, she had thought about going back to Willow Oak to get Ruth to talk more, but remembering the scowl on her face kept Bethany from even attempting.

She couldn't force the woman to have a relationship with her, no matter how much she wanted to. She reminded herself of the old saying, *time heals all wounds*, and she wondered if that would be true in her case. At least she still had her father.

Her father. Bethany thought back to the older man. A few months ago, when she had first planned the trip from New York to Redwood, she had thought her father had attempted to intervene because of jealousy. Now, she knew he had been trying to protect her in his own way. She had sent him a telegram inviting him to her wedding, but she had not received a message back. Perhaps he was still mad at her. Suppose he didn't forgive her? Perhaps she and Peter could make a trip to New York after the wedding.

"After we finish your wedding dress, we should think about your nightclothes. Especially for your wedding night. Any ideas?" Penelope threw her a mischievous smile.

"I want something fancy," Bethany admitted. If she were back in New York, her wedding clothes and the things for her trousseau would have been made by the most talented modiste money could buy. But supplies in Wisconsin were limited, and although there was a modiste in town, her work didn't come close to the kind Imogene could do. "Maybe with a high-necked collar."

"I don't think you should bother with a nightgown at all," Imogene replied saucily. "It's going to end up on the floor."

Penelope laughed. "When did you start being so

daring? This is coming from a woman who had to receive the wedding night talk from her own mother-in-law."

"Precisely," Imogene admitted, not looking the least bit embarrassed. "Now that Bethany doesn't have to worry about the wedding night, she no longer has to worry about securing the nightclothes for the wedding night."

"I still want a nightgown. I can't walk around naked, can I?"

Penelope snorted. "I'm sure Peter wouldn't mind."

The comment reminded Bethany of the fact she and Peter hadn't made love in quite a while, and she was starting to get frustrated with her fiancé. "Truthfully, I feel Peter still sees me as a patient rather than a fiancée. I adore him, but his constant fussing is on the verge of driving me mad, and since I got ill, we haven't—"

"You haven't what?"

Penelope studied Bethany's flushed face. "Is Peter being difficult about making love to you just because you were sick?"

"Yes." Bethany bit her lower lip. "I appreciate his concern, but he is acting as if I were at death's door."

"Well, you were quite sick, Beth," Imogene told her gently. "Perhaps, he is just trying to be a bit careful so that you don't overexert yourself before the wedding."

"But still, I've been better for days." Bethany sighed. "It's just that after you've experienced lovemaking, you cannot go back to how things were. I'm amazed some women do not simply go feral without it."

"Trust me, not all men are as you imagine they are in the marriage bed. When you find one who can actually bring you pleasure, you'd do good to hold tight and never let go," Penelope blurted out. "Excuse me, I am going to nurse Colin."

Imogene laughed. "I expect a lot of babies in Penelope and Derek's future. Those two are crazy over each other." She looked at her. "What about you, Bethany? Do you want children?"

"I've always wanted a daughter," she confessed. "I never had any siblings growing up, and it's lonely business being an only child. But if Peter keeps living like a priest, that will never happen."

Imogene patted her hand. "Don't worry about Peter. He'll come around. You'll see, once he knows you are as right as rain. I've been married for two years, Bethany, and believe me when I say men are not as complicated as they seem."

She raised an eyebrow as she looked at her curiously. "Are you saying I should seduce him?" Bethany supposed she could try that; she had always been a good flirt. She suspected Peter was just as eager as she was to make love. She guessed she had a few tricks up her sleeve to encourage her almost-husband to make love to her.

Her almost sister-in-law laughed. "I am saying nothing of the sort, but by the look in your eyes, I think you have your own plans. Can I offer a piece of advice? Wait until tomorrow to try whatever trick you're planning."

"Why?"

"Because those three men are going to be as drunk as skunks tonight, well, perhaps not Derek. I assure you, Peter is going to be much easier to manage tomorrow."

The three Stevenson brothers clinked their glasses containing whisky, the first of many, merrily. Stefan took the first sip as he pointed the glass to his eldest brother. "To my brother, Peter, who will finally have someone else calling all the shots."

Derek snorted as he started drinking. "Over his dead body."

Peter ignored their teasing. "Happy to say that I can't wait for someone to henpeck me." He raised his hand, motioning to the barkeeper to send him another drink. He knew he should probably be slowing down, as he did have to work tomorrow, but he was just so damn happy.

He and Bethany would be getting married, and he no longer had to worry about Bethany running all over Wisconsin trying to win the approval of a woman who didn't even want her. Not that Peter didn't feel sorry for how things had turned out, but he had always believed that it was better to be alone than in bad company, and if Ruth didn't want to be a part of Bethany's life, then it was her loss.

Stefan turned to look at Derek. "Isn't it some type of sin to drink on the evening before Sunday?"

"Don't be such a rule follower, Stefan. I invited Derek to have a good time, and I won't have you spoiling all the fun."

"I'm only having one glass, in honor of our brother," Derek said firmly as he cocked his head in Peter's direction. "Believe me, it's not me you should be worried about. He had three glasses before either of us could get here."

Peter finished his drink. "I could always hold my liquor better than you two could. Don't tell me you both are done after one measly drink."

"I have church in the morning," Derek responded primly.

"Not to mention, a headache that is going to feel a lot worse if there is a baby crying," Stefan quipped. "Derek and I are all right with one glass."

"Cowards." Peter finished off their drinks. There was no way he was going to let his younger brothers ruin his mood. "I am more than happy to keep on celebrating by myself. Bethany Fields is the best thing that has ever happened to me in my life and if I could marry her right now, I would. Cheers."

The next morning, however, Peter was feeling less than merry. So much so, that he didn't bother attending church, despite his mother's obvious frown. He wanted nothing more than to crawl into bed, but both of his deputies had sent word that they were sick, so he had no choice but to sit in the sheriff's office.

Peter took a sip of his coffee and made a face. It was only making him feel worse. There was a knock on the door and his fiancée came in looking bright and pretty while he looked quite miserable. She was wearing a thick green dress that matched her eyes and had paired it off with a bonnet that had a silk ribbon tied under her chin. She had told him his mother had bought it for her as a wedding present. His mother was very obviously overjoyed at the prospect of having another daughter-in-law.

"How are you feeling?" Bethany asked as she closed the door. Then she started covering the windows with the beige curtains that had been in the office for the last ten years.

"Honestly, worse." His dreaded headache was momentarily gone as he looked at her curiously. "What on earth are you doing, my dear?"

"Giving us some privacy."

She had an odd look on her face, a mix between being mischievous and being daring. Peter was curious. "Won't anyone come looking for you?"

"I told your parents you would give me a ride back to

the house because I had something I needed to discuss with you about the wedding."

"What if there is an emergency and someone is in dire need of my services?"

"Then they can wait."

"You won't make a very good sheriff's wife."

"Just like I wasn't a very good teacher; thankfully, I'm a much better student."

Before Peter could ask what she meant by that, Bethany was on her knees. He gave her a perplexed look, only half knowing where this was going. They hadn't made love in quite a while, since before she had found her mother. At first, it was because she had been sick, then while she had been recuperating, he had thought it would be nice to wait until their wedding night. Apparently, his almost-wife did not think the same way.

For a woman who had been a virgin in bed, she unbuckled his belt and pulled down his trousers with ease. She raised her head innocently. "Penny taught me about this trick last night. I want to see if it will work."

"We should wait," he protested weakly, and he couldn't convince even himself. "We are getting married in just a matters of days."

"Just relax," she purred, sounding more seductive than any whore he had even lain with. "I want to make you feel good, just like you always do to me."

Peter wanted to protest. They should wait until the wedding night after all, but he would be lying if he said he wasn't rock hard already. Not to mention, he had been dying to get her into bed since she recuperated. He had managed to hold back out of sheer willpower.

She parted her lips and slowly started accepting his rapidly hardening cock inside her mouth. It was a miracle Peter didn't finish inside her the second he felt the warmth of her mouth and tongue on him. He made a mental note to thank Penny later for her advice, even if the thought of the girls talking about their love lives caused a chill to go down his spine. And here, he had thought they only spoke about hair ribbons and housekeeping.

Her movements were slow and calculating, which didn't surprise him. She was still a beginner. Ever the generous soul, he decided to help her out. "Take as much as you can, sweetheart," he murmured as he ran a hand through her blonde locks. "Then when you're ready, you can play with your tongue."

She looked at him with confusion.

"Swirl your tongue around my manhood. Play around with it." He could feel himself blush as if he were a young man again, feeling awkward giving such directions to Bethany. On second thought, he was going to tattle to Derek for having Penny corrupt his young bride.

He soon forgot about Penny, when Bethany started doing what he had told her to do. Her first movements were a bit odd as she tried to get used to the sensation of moving her tongue with his cock inside her mouth, but she soon found herself growing in confidence.

Her pink tongue swirled around the base of his cock as she coated every inch of it with her tongue. Her lips were pressed firmly against his member as she slowly started pleasuring him with her mouth. She pulled back, only to take him all at once a second later, with her green eyes as big as saucers. It felt as if his cock were inside a tight, enclosed place that was milking him slowly. Peter couldn't believe how her mouth could make him weak at the knees.

He couldn't hold on any longer and felt himself finish inside her mouth. His seed spilled from inside her surprised little mouth as he gripped the desk to steady himself. He could get quite used to this. Though, next time, it would probably be best to do it in the privacy of their own home, but he did admire her spontaneity.

Once Peter felt his heart stop racing, he looked back at his fiancée, who had a content look on her face, reminding Peter of a cat who ate the canary. Her lips were shiny and plump, and the bonnet had slipped from her head to her shoulders.

Peter gripped her by the waist and placed her on his desk, her delightful squeals music to his ears. Up came her dress and endless amounts of petticoats and whatever frills were under it and down came her drawers.

He cupped her pussy in his hand, and he chuckled when he felt the warmness between her legs. She was gushing into his palm almost immediately. "You're practically drenched, baby," he growled into her ear. "You are going to leave my desk covered in your wetness."

Bethany blushed as she tried to hide her face against her shoulder. For someone so sassy, she could be shy when she wanted to be. Peter hoped she was always like that because he loved watching her blush.

"No, no, Miss Fields, don't hide from me. You were feeling quite cocky earlier, were you not?" His fingers touched the soft pad of her flesh through her blonde curls as he started heading towards her clit which, no doubt, was eager for his touch. "Are you wet because you enjoyed having my cock between your lips?"

Bethany only whimpered in need.

He started tracing his fingers between her sensitive inner thighs. "Answer me, darling."

"Yes."

"Use your words, sweetheart," he ordered as he pulled on both legs, sliding her butt down on the hard desk in order to pull her farther towards him. "Do you want me to bury the cock you just pleasured with your pretty little mouth inside you?"

Bethany had started panting, and her cheeks had turned an adorable pink color against her pale complexion. She spread her legs farther apart, as if giving him an answer, and Peter looked on in need at her dewy, plump little lips.

He gripped her hips as he tried not to grab hard enough to bruise her. His cock started opening her lips as he felt the tightness around it. He grunted, loving that feeling. It felt like his manhood was being wrapped in velvet.

Bethany somehow managed to grip both edges of his desk while she started sliding her back up and down as he started thrusting into her. Every time he entered her, she would pull back teasingly with a sly smile on her face. She was so seductive that Peter wasn't even annoyed that she was teasing him when he felt he was about to burst.

The little minx gripped the bodice on her dress and managed to pull down the tight ruffles to expose a pair of soft breasts with rose-colored nipples. The little seductress started playing with her breasts in front of him, squeezing them, pinching them, so there were fingernail marks on them, and twisting her hard little nipples until they nearly turned red from the torture she was inflicting on them.

Peter thrust into her as she continued to play with herself, then her hands moved from her breasts to the love button between her thighs as her almost-husband continued to bury himself inside her tight quim. He wished he could feel like this always, feeling her hot little body under him, the feeling of her pussy squeezing every last drop of his seed from him, and her breasts rubbing against his chest.

"Oh, Peter, I do so love you," she announced in a

breathy whisper as she wrapped her arms around his neck. It was all he needed to finish inside her.

Peter's entire body was trembling, and he only managed to continue standing by sheer force of will. There was a knock on the door, and he let out a loud hiss, letting them know he was indisposed. He turned to his fiancée, who was rearranging the bodice of her dress. "I'm afraid the fun is over, sweetheart. Let's get dressed."

Chapter 13

Bethany couldn't remember the last time she had felt so nervous. The thing was she wasn't quite sure what she was feeling nervous about. But she supposed all brides felt apprehensive on the day before their wedding, even brides who were sure about marrying their grooms.

Between Imogene, Penelope, and herself, they had managed to finish the pink dress with the large sash for the wedding, and even though it wasn't white, she looked exquisite in it if she did say so herself. She had been trying it on to make sure it fit for tomorrow and no last-minute alterations were needed.

Everything was prepared and going according to plan. Derek would be marrying them at his church. Daisy would be their flower girl, and Colin, the ringbearer, with both of them being carried by their mothers since neither of them could walk. Her in-laws were hosting a small reception back at their home. By the end of the day tomorrow, she would be the newest Mrs. Stevenson, and she and Peter would be living in their own home in town.

There was a knock on the door, and she smoothed down her dress. It was probably Mrs. Stevenson wanting to see if there was anything that needed to be fixed "Come in, Mrs. Stevenson."

It occurred to Bethany that only the Stevenson family would be present at the wedding tomorrow. Bethany's father hadn't responded to the telegram she'd sent him. The wedding had been on such short notice, she wasn't sure if her father would even be able to attend or if he had forgiven her already. She asked Mr. Stevenson to walk her down the aisle and the older gentleman had agreed.

"Hello, sweet pea."

Bethany gasped as she turned around and saw her father standing there in a dusty traveling suit. "Daddy!" She hugged him tightly, not caring that she was probably covering her dress with dust and dirt. "You came! I wasn't sure if you were going to be able to make it."

Edwin Fields chuckled as he kissed her cheek. "And miss the wedding of my little girl? Never. I've been traveling for the past few days, and I've never been more exhausted in my life. But it was worth it, to see how pretty and happy you look right now."

Bethany's lower lip trembled as she hugged him again. "Oh, Daddy, thank you for coming." The sad look in her father's eyes told Bethany he knew what had happened with Ruth based on her letter, and now she knew her father keeping her mother away from her hadn't been an act of cruelty, but one of kindness. "How did you find the house?"

"I asked someone in town. Your future mother-in-law opened the door. Nice woman."

"Yes, she is."

He cleared his throat. "I take it you met your mother." She nodded sadly. "I wish I could say something to make you feel better, Bethany. The truth is I don't have anything. Your mother, well, she never wanted to be a mother. I should have told you that from the start, before you made the long journey here alone."

Bethany shook her head. "Oh, Daddy, you don't have to apologize. If I had never come to Redwood, I wouldn't have ever met Peter, and that would have been the true tragedy. You haven't met him yet, but he really is a wonderful man."

"I'm sure he is if you chose him to be your husband." Mr. Fields studied her closely. "You've grown up quite nicely, honey. You seem more mature and wiser than you did back in New York. Maybe this little trip did do you good after all. Now how about you take me to meet the man who is going to be your husband?"

Bethany nodded. "He's at work right now, but we can walk to town together. Oh, Daddy, I'm so glad you're going to be here for my wedding."

Mr. Fields kissed her on the cheek, his voice breaking slightly. "Me too, honey."

In the end, Penelope and Imogene had been right, and the pink dress looked absolutely perfect for a simple, morning wedding. It fit like a glove, and between her and Penelope, they had even managed to make a large sash around the waist from the extra material leftover from the dress. Imogene had added small imitation rosebuds imported all the way from England along the collar of her dress and the sleeves. Bethany had been surprised that their small general store had actually managed to have something as fancy as fake rosebuds in stock. They were currently all the rage in New York, Imogene promised, according to the knowledge she got from newspapers and ladies' magazines, and so much more practical than fresh flowers which were nearly impossible to find in December.

Mrs. Stevenson had let her borrow a brooch made out of real gold, and her father's wedding present to her had been a pair of beautiful diamond earrings that would shine every time the light hit them. Her bouquet consisted of pink roses tied with a white ribbon that exactly matched the shade of pink of her dress.

Derek was ready to perform the ceremony, and Imogene and Penelope were ready with their children, to walk down the aisle as the flower girl and ring bearer respectively. Her in-laws, along with a couple of Peter's friends, were already sitting in the pews, and with any luck, Peter was at the altar waiting for her.

Everything was going according to plan, so why was she so nervous? She had been pacing around the room for the past ten minutes, not sure what she was doing. She had dismissed Mrs. Stevenson, Penelope, and Imogene, telling them she needed a few minutes to collect herself; now she wished she hadn't kicked them out.

Peter. She needed to talk to Peter. Perhaps that would put her mind at ease. Yes, talking to Peter would make all this nervousness go away. She glanced at the ancient-looking clock in the room and noticed there was still twenty minutes until the ceremony began and for her father to come and collect her. Twenty minutes was more than enough.

She slightly opened the door of the room she was staying in at the back of the church, where she was getting ready, and peeked out. She saw Imogene fussing over baby Daisy's dress and then she saw Derek and Penelope talking to Peter.

Bethany stopped in her tracks as she looked at her

future husband. She was so used to seeing him in his rough work clothes that it felt odd seeing him in something more formal. He was wearing a dark gray suit that clung to every muscle perfectly and accented his best features. His dark hair was combed back, and he was clean-shaven. Unlike his bride, he looked at ease, as if he had been waiting for this moment his entire life.

"Peter!" she whispered, urging him to come forward, not caring if it was bad luck that a groom saw his bride before the wedding. "Come here."

Peter immediately had a concerned look on his face as he did as he was told. Once he was safely inside, she shut the door quickly.

Before she could even explain, he gripped her by the shoulders as if to steady her. He started talking rapidly. "What is it? What's wrong? Are you sick? I knew we shouldn't have hurried things before—"

In order to get him to stop rambling, Bethany pressed her lips against his, kissing him. Peter relaxed slightly as he started running his hands across her back. "Well, good morning to you too," he murmured. "I must admit, Miss Fields, I didn't expect to see you for the first time in your wedding dress, hiding in a room at the back of the church."

Bethany rolled her eyes playfully. "That is not the reason why I called you down here."

Peter raised an eyebrow in curiosity. "Now, why did you drag me here minutes before the ceremony is supposed to start? You know how Derek feels about punctuality."

"I..." she trailed off as she blurted out, "aren't you nervous about getting married?"

"No, though to be honest, I am older than you. I should have been married a long time ago."

"Then you wouldn't have married me."

"That's right, then I wouldn't be married to you. And what a tragedy that would be." He smiled at her as he held her hand and led her back to the nearby settee. "Come, Beth, and talk to me." Once they were both seated, he turned to face her. "Now tell me, what is going on in that beautiful mind of yours?"

"I'm just nervous," she admitted, then she quickly said, "not that I am having second thoughts, but just this entire ordeal. I came to Redwood to find my mother, and never in a million years, did I think I would find the man I would spend the rest of my life with."

Peter kissed her sweetly as he nibbled on her bottom lip. "How sweet, you're going to make me cry."

Bethany rolled her eyes as she cupped his face in her hands. "I am being serious. Even though my mother ended up rejecting me, I am so happy that I met you, Peter. You have changed my life in the most incredible way."

"That woman is going to regret the decision of not being involved in your life every second of her life." Peter pressed her head against his shoulder. "You are a hard-working, determined young woman, Bethany Fields. Not to mention, sassy, with a good, loving heart. I am proud to call you my wife."

Bethany smiled as she cuddled against his chest. "You are a pretty fine man yourself, Peter Stevenson, even though you like to drive me nuts with your teasing."

"You love that I tease you." Peter bit her lower earlobe gently as he patted her bottom. "Now, how about we get our wedding started? The last thing we want is to keep our guests waiting."

She nodded as he helped her up. She stared at him with big, round, green eyes. "Peter, we are going to be very happy, aren't we?"

Peter lifted both of her hands together and kissed

them. "Bethany Fields, I say with much certainty that you and I are going to be very happy for a very long time."

"Daisy, honey, please don't fall asleep." Imogene looked at her nearly sleeping daughter wearing the blue and white dress that she had painstakingly sewn together just for the ceremony. Unfortunately for her, Daisy, Peter and Bethany's flower girl, had decided at that moment that it was the perfect time to take a nap.

Imogene sighed. She understood it wasn't a big deal. She had been planning on carrying Daisy down the aisle while she threw rose petals on the church's floor, but still, she'd wanted the baby to at least be awake.

"Looks like you lost that round, Imogene." Stefan rested his chin on her shoulder as he looked down proudly at his sleeping daughter. "She is out like a candle. You are not going to get her to wake up for the ceremony."

"Perhaps not." Imogene sighed. "Should I wake her?"

"I wouldn't unless you want to deal with a screaming baby all through the ceremony." Stefan smiled. "She looks adorable when she's sleeping. She's going to look just like you when she grows up."

Imogene snorted. "I hope not."

Stefan pinched her on the butt.

"Ow, what was that for?"

"I won't have you giving yourself ill remarks," he scolded. "You're beautiful. Always have been, and always will be. Just because those people from the dreary little town you came from made you feel different, doesn't mean it's true. Understood?"

"Yes, sir," she grumbled. In an effort to lighten the

mood, she looked up at her husband. "Do you remember our wedding day?"

He nodded as he wrapped his arms around his wife and started rocking both his wife and infant daughter back and forth. "I remember; we hardly knew each other back then."

"Two years," she mused. "How on earth does time go by so fast? Now all of us are happily married. I'm happy for Peter. I think Bethany will be a good fit for him."

"I think so too. She keeps him on his toes. Like someone I know."

"I didn't leave town several times without any supervision."

"No, my dear, you only almost committed attempted murder."

"I did no such thing. I told you it was an accident." She saw that Stefan was laughing at her and she scowled. "You're teasing me. You really can be quite horrid when you want to be."

"Only because you're so innocent, my love." He kissed her forehead before his lips started trailing down towards her slightly exposed collarbone, for once, not caring that there was an audience a mere few feet away. "How about after the ceremony, we skip the reception and go back home, put the baby down for a nap, and celebrate that my older brother finally got married?"

Imogene had been about to protest when she noticed the smirk on his face. "Oh, you're teasing me again."

"Only part of that sentence is teasing, my wife," he admitted. "We can still have our celebration long after the reception is finally over."

"Oh?" She raised an eyebrow curiously. "And what would that celebration include?"

Stefan tilted her chin up so he could kiss her with ease. "Anything you want, Mrs. Stevenson."

———

Derek gave an exaggerated sigh as he looked at his pocket watch while he tapped his foot impatiently. "They're late. What on earth could be taking them so long? I'll just go and get them myself."

"I wouldn't do that." Penelope looked exasperated as she tried to calm a fussy baby Colin. "Not unless you want to catch your sister-in-law in a compromising position."

Derek's hazel eyes widened as he ran his hand through his combed hair. "They wouldn't! Not in a church for Heaven's sake. It's immoral."

"Aren't you remembering all of the potentially sinful things we've done since we first married, husband?" Penelope had a fake smile on her face, in case anyone thought something was amiss. "I'm sure Peter and Bethany engaging in marital bliss mere minutes before their wedding is not anything we can judge them for."

Derek reddened. "It's different."

"How so?"

"Well, for starters, we never did it on church property."

"No." A familiar smirk appeared on Penelope's delicate face. "But we did do it in several other places that perhaps not everyone thought proper."

Derek murmured something under his breath as he picked up Colin and tried to soothe him. "I suppose we can give them a few more minutes, but we need to get them out of there soon. Otherwise, my parents and Bethany's father are sure to notice something is wrong, and then both of them are going to be more embarrassed."

Penelope rubbed his forearm. "Stop worrying. You will

give yourself gray hairs."

"Then if you want to prevent that, tell Peter and Bethany to come out so I can actually start the ceremony."

She ignored his comment. "Are we going to dance this afternoon at the reception?"

"Surely not."

Penelope fluttered her eyelashes. "Please? I haven't danced in so long."

Derek finally sighed. "I can never say no to you, can I?"

"No, you cannot. Three dances."

"One dance."

"Two dances."

"Fine," Derek finally agreed as he kissed her. "Two dances, and that is it. Don't make me humiliate myself further."

"I don't know why you think you're such a horrible dancer. You are quite decent. I did teach you myself."

"I've never enjoyed dancing," he admitted. "Unless I am dancing with you."

Penelope smiled. "I'm fine with only one dance, as long as I'm your only partner,"

"Mrs. Stevenson, you are the only partner I want."

The door of the small room at the back of the church flew open and Bethany and Peter came outside. Almost immediately, Derek reverted himself to his strict pastor persona. "You're late. The ceremony should have started already."

"Well, I'm here." Peter cleared his throat. "Let's go together. Penny, can you round up Imogene and Daisy? I'll tell Mr. Fields that Beth is ready."

Penny nodded. "Sure thing." She turned to Bethany. "Are you ready?"

Bethany clutched her bridal bouquet in her hands. "I've never felt more ready."

Chapter 14

"**Y**ou may kiss your bride."

Bethany Fields, now Stevenson, had to bite her cheek to keep from laughing as she turned to stare at her new husband. She had been feeling giddy all morning, except for those brief moments when her nerves had gotten the best of her, but after she and Peter had talked, she had returned back to her happy self. Imogene told her it was probably from all the excitement. Bethany wasn't sure what it was, exactly. All she knew was that she felt much happier than she'd been in a long time.

Peter cocked an eyebrow at her in amusement as he pulled up her veil. He looked handsome in his suit, and he reminded Bethany of the boys back in New York. She preferred him when he was wearing his hat, his roughened clothes, and riding a horse. She mentally reminded herself to tease him about this later.

"Why are you giggling, my new bride?" he managed to murmur as he looked at her as if the answer was written on her face. His hazel eyes shone brightly as he looked at her with his lips curled in a familiar smirk.

Bethany gave a simple shrug as she stood on her tippy-toes so that he could kiss her more easily. "I'm just so happy."

"Not as happy as I am."

With that last, bold statement, her new husband pulled her in for a kiss. His hand was resting on her lower back as he tilted her back to kiss her even deeper. Around them, loud cheers erupted as the couple finished kissing.

Once they finally pulled apart, Peter gripped her hand as they started exiting the church. She caught her father's eye as he blew her a kiss. He was going back to New York by the end of the week, and he had made Bethany and Peter promise they would visit soon. Even though it was technically her honeymoon period, she wanted to spend as much time with her father as she could, that is if her new husband would even let her leave their bed.

Peter helped her into the wagon and once Bethany was seated firmly on the seat, they waved back to their guests. They were supposed to head back to the elder Stevenson home for the wedding reception.

But when Bethany saw him driving in the opposite direction, she turned to stare at him. "Where on earth are we going? Your mother is going to kill us if we are late to our reception party."

"We have time for a detour." There was a slight smirk on his lips as he parked the wagon in front of his house. No, *their* house. It was a lovely home, with two spare bedrooms in addition to the main bedroom. Plenty of room for a nursery or two, Mrs. Stevenson had pointed out, which caused Bethany to giggle and Peter to groan when his mother had mentioned it.

There were still some things Bethany wanted to add, to make it homier for both of them. The first thing, of course, that she was going to do was remove those awful couches in the sitting room and then—

The new Mrs. Stevenson let out a surprised gasp when her new husband pulled her into his arms as he carried her, bridal style, into their house. She could feel the blush coating her cheeks. "Just what on earth are you planning, Peter Stevenson?"

"I'm planning on making love to my beautiful wife until I hear her cry out in pleasure, over and over again." Peter nibbled on her ear. "Is that a good enough reason for you, Beth?"

Bethany laughed as she curled her head on the crook of his neck. "Well, I suppose we can take a few minutes to celebrate our marriage."

Peter leaned down to kiss her. "Music to my ears, Mrs. Stevenson."

"Peter, I want a baby."

Peter stopped dead in his tracks to stare at his wife of just a few minutes. For once, Bethany had rendered him speechless as he turned to stare at her. "What?"

Bethany laughed shyly at his dumbfounded expression. "I know we didn't really discuss it, but I just thought it would be nice to have a baby. We are properly married now, after all, and we were quite lucky before, not getting pregnant, considering all the times we did it."

"Wow, a baby." Peter repeated, "A baby."

He had never thought much about having a child with Bethany. He had been too busy the past few weeks, helping her get better and getting her down the aisle, to think about the prospect of having children. Peter thought back to his niece and nephew whom he adored, and the thought of having his own child with Bethany who, perhaps, would have her green eyes made his heart swell.

Bethany looked concerned. "You don't want a baby?"

"No, of course, I do. You just caught me by surprise, darling."

"I just thought it would be the sensible thing to do. You're getting older and my father is, as well, and I'm not working as a teacher any longer. I thought a baby would be really nice. Daisy and Colin could have another cousin. Maybe it's all the excitement about the wedding and becoming part of the Stevenson family, but I want a baby. I know it's God's plan and all and we might not even have children, but still, I think we ought—"

Peter stopped her rambling by pulling her into a kiss. "Honey, stop before you make yourself dizzy. I think a baby is a wonderful idea, and we will have as many babies as God wants us to have." He squeezed her rump. "Though I don't appreciate being called old, young lady."

Bethany giggled. "You don't look a day over thirty, darling."

Peter chuckled at her teasing as he carried her up the stairs. "I'll tell you the same thing, honey, when you turn thirty-eight." He kissed her. "Now, we need to hurry upstairs if we're going to make a baby by next year."

Bethany burst into giggles as she wrapped her arms around his neck. "Peter Stevenson, we are going to have so much fun making this baby."

"Oh, do you have a few tricks up your sleeve, Mrs. Stevenson?"

"A few. I'm sure you have more that you can teach me."

"It would be my pleasure."

Epilogue

One year later...

"**B**ethany!"

Imogene Stevenson looked up from where she was rocking Daisy to sleep. She raised an eyebrow toward her mother-in-law who was knitting a pair of baby booties. Three Stevenson women were currently on the porch of the elder Mrs. Stevenson's home while the fourth one was a few feet away. "Is this the third time he's called her name?"

Mrs. Stevenson shrugged, not at all concerned by her eldest son yelling his wife's name. "Fourth time, I believe."

Penelope snorted. She was resting on her knees, playing with her son, Colin. She removed the toy soldier that Colin stuffed in his mouth. She looked towards where Peter was nearly stomping in search of his wife. "He's going to be hoarse by the time the baby arrives, and he still has five months to go."

"Babies," Imogene corrected, her face containing a mix of amusement and sympathy. "And they might come sooner. Dr. Moore says it's tricky with twins. The good thing is Bethany still has her fighting spirit. Poor Peter."

"Do we even know if it's twins yet?"

Mrs. Stevenson shrugged. "Well, Dr. Moore says you can never be one hundred percent sure. Even in these modern times, but Bethany's pregnancy is advancing rapidly and there is quite a lot of movement in her belly."

"Not to mention, she's huge," Penelope blurted out as she looked over her shoulder toward where Bethany and Peter were at each other's throats. "I'm surprised she's still moving around."

"Peter has been trying to keep her still, but Bethany is Bethany. I'm afraid his hair will go gray by the time she gives birth."

"Do you think the house will be done by then?" Imogene inquired. Bethany's father had given then quite a large sum of money as a wedding present. Bethany and Peter had decided to use the money to build a house on Stevenson property. They wanted their children to have a safe place to play and grow up with their aunt, uncle, and grandparents just a few feet away.

"Oh, I think so. There is no one faster than the Daryll brothers. They should be done in a month or so."

"Do you think we should say anything?" Penelope pointed toward the squabbling couple a few feet away.

Imogene shook her head. "You don't want to get in the middle of that, believe me. It's better if you just let them squabble it out."

"What the hell are you doing?" Peter thought he had asked the question at least thirty-two times in the past four days, but by the way it was going with his wife, he might as well be speaking to the damn wall.

Peter took the piece of wood from his heavily pregnant wife's hands, barely resisting the urge to bend her over his knee and give her a spanking she wouldn't forget anytime soon. When Bethany had told him she was pregnant months earlier, he had been thrilled. Not only because he was finally becoming a father, but because he hoped it would mean Bethany would settle down to the serene role of wife and mother.

In an act of cruel irony, Bethany Stevenson had become even more restless, constantly fussing over things and hardly sitting down for more than ten minutes. Usually, her attempts were harmless enough—redecorating the nursery for the fourth time, attempting to knit baby blankets, cleaning and then recleaning the house. But ever since the Daryll brothers and their team of workers had started building their new home, she had become even more fidgety. She didn't seem too concerned about the fact she was very possibly carrying twins in her belly. She still tried to "help" out. He had never thought he would have to pry wood, a hammer, and nails, among other things, out of his wife's hands.

"Are you out of your mind?" he snapped as he tossed the piece of wood aside. "You're pregnant. You're going to hurt the baby if you don't keep still."

"Babies," Bethany corrected with a bored expression. She had gotten significantly cockier ever since Peter had told her he wouldn't be spanking her while she was expecting. "And I'm just trying to help."

Peter took in a deep breath, trying to keep the famous Stevenson temper in check. "They don't need your help; that's why we're paying them." His mother had told him women often felt restless and eager to get the house ready for the arrival of their babies. When his mother had told him this, he sure as hell hadn't thought Bethany would be trying to build the house herself.

Bethany pouted at him, and before she could argue, he snatched her arm and pulled her away from the construction team. He pulled her in for a kiss as he grumbled, "What am I going to do with you?"

"Love me?" Bethany blinked innocently as she rested her hand on her pregnant belly. Maybe Dr. Moore was right, and she was expecting twins. Good grief.

"Or spank you, more likely." Peter raised a dark eyebrow as he reached down and squeezed one plump buttock.

"Don't," she gasped as she settled her head against his chest. "You promised."

"And you promised not to turn my hair gray or give me a heart attack, yet here we are."

She gave him a serene smile. "You would look very handsome with gray hair. I just want everything to be perfect for you, for us, for our children. Don't you?"

"Of course, I do," Peter insisted as he waved a finger in her direction. "Which is why I'm supervising the workers. What I don't need, my darling wife, is your meddling. You could get hurt. Promise me you won't come back to the property until the house is complete."

"I can hardly avoid it. We are staying with your parents, after all, until the house is finished."

"I meant, you need to stay out of the construction area, my darling girl. You won't like the consequences if I catch you here again trying to build the house by yourself. Understood?"

"I'm tired," Bethany said instead, as they began walking to the elder Stevenson's home. "I'm going to take a nap."

"Bethany!" he growled.

"Oh, all right, you grump. I promise. But if the house doesn't meet your expectations, don't blame it on me. I was only trying to help."

"I wouldn't dream of it." Peter pulled her in for another kiss. "Thank you. I love you."

Bethany softened as she caressed his face with her soft hands. "I love you more."

Four and a half months later, Bethany Stevenson, nee Fields, gave birth to two healthy twin girls. The doting mother promptly named her blonde-haired twins Francesca and Fiorella. Much to her husband Peter Stevenson's delight and somewhat horror, they turned out to be exactly like his wife.

Annabelle Marin

Annabelle Marin is a twenty-something romantic who lives in sunny California. When she isn't writing she enjoys daydreaming, watching way too much TV, and cuddling with her pets.

Her books are sweet erotic romances with domestic discipline. In her books you can expect: a spoonful of sweetness, a dash of sass, a cup of naughtiness, and an abundance of romance.

You can follow Annabelle on Facebook, Instagram, Goodreads, and Bookbub for exciting updates on upcoming books!

Facebook-https://www.facebook.com/annabelle.
marin.940/
Instagram-https://www.
instagram.com/missannabellemarin/
Bookbub-//www.bookbub.com/profile/annabelle-marin
Goodreads-www.goodreads.com/author/show/
21061973.Annabelle_Marin

Don't miss these exciting titles by Annabelle Marin and Blushing Books!

Endless Paradise
Between Kisses & Lies

The Stevenson Brothers Series

The Rancher Orders a Bride
The Pastor Takes a Wife
The Sheriff Finds a Fiancée

Vintage Beauties Series
Bless Her Heart

The Bride Series
The Unwilling Mrs.
The Unattainable Bride
The Unexpected Wife

Anthologies
12 Naughty Days of Christmas 2021

Blushing Books

Blushing Books is the oldest eBook publisher on the web. We've been running websites that publish steamy romance and erotica since 1999, and we have been selling eBooks since 2003. We have free and promotional offerings that change weekly, so please do visit us at http://www.blushingbooks.com/free.

Blushing Books Newsletter

Please join the Blushing Books newsletter
to receive updates & special promotional offers.
You can also join by using your mobile phone:
Just text BLUSHING to 22828.

Every month, one new sign up via text messaging will
receive a $25.00 Amazon gift card, so sign up today!